The Batter Witch Project

Sue Hollowell

The Batter Witch Project

Cover by Melody Simmons at bookcoversbymelody.com

Contents

Chapter 1

The flickering candlelight at Rosemary's Table cast dancing shadows across Jake's face. I couldn't help but notice how the warm glow softened his usually rugged features. My fingers fidgeted with the cloth napkin in my lap as I tried to convince myself this wasn't really a date—even though it absolutely was. The restaurant, a converted Victorian farmhouse just outside Starfall Glen, had been Jake's choice, and I had to admit he'd picked perfectly.

Exposed wooden beams, weathered to a rich honey color by decades of use, crossed the ceiling above us. Fairy lights twinkled between potted herbs on the deep windowsills, their soft glow reflecting off the antique glass panes.

Our table, tucked into a cozy alcove beneath an arched window, felt like our own private world. The white tablecloth glowed warmly in the candlelight. And someone had arranged fresh wildflowers in a delicate blue mason jar between us. It was exactly thethe place my grandfather would have loved—full of character and stories, just waiting to be discovered.

At my feet, Pecan shifted, his furry body pressed against my ankle in silent support. *You're overthinking again, Maple. He's already looked at you exactly seventeen times since we sat down. I'd say that's a good sign. Though he's also thinking about whether he has engine grease under his fingernails, which is adorably nervous of him. And yes, he checked them three times in the truck before coming in.*

I fought back a smile at my dog's narration. Having a mind-reading Tibetan Terrier came with its perks, though sometimes his running commentary was more distracting than helpful. Especially when I was trying to focus on not making a fool of myself during my first real date with Jake.

The journey to this moment had been anything but straightforward. For months, Jake had been fixing my grandfather's old Waffle Wagon, turning what started as simple maintenance calls into longer visits filled with coffee and conversation. I'd inherited both the truck and my grandfather's famous waffle recipes six months ago, and while the recipes were perfect, the truck had seen better days.

He spent extra time on those repairs, you know, Pecan had told me more than once. *He could have fixed that radiator in two hours, but he stretched it to four just to talk to you.*

"You look really nice tonight, Maple." Jake's voice was warm honey over rough gravel, and I felt heat rise to my cheeks. He'd cleaned up nicely himself, trading his usual work clothes for dark jeans and a blue button-down that made his eyes look even more striking than usual. A hint of his usual motor oil scent lingered beneath his cologne, and somehow that made him even more appealing.

"Thank you." I tucked a loose strand of hair behind my ear, grateful that Sarah had talked me into wearing it down instead of my usual practical ponytail. "Lucky's niece actually helped me pick this outfit. I think she had way too much fun dragging me around town." I gestured down at my flowing blouse and skirt combination, remembering how Sarah had practically squealed when I emerged from the dressing room.

Jake's eyes lingered on me, making my heart do a little skip. "Well, she did a great job. You look beautiful." His fingers drummed lightly on the table, a nervous gesture I'd noticed whenever he was working up to saying something. "Actually, I've been wanting to ask you out for a while now."

Three months, two weeks, and four days, Pecan chimed in. *I've been counting. His thoughts get all mushy whenever he sees you in the Waffle Wagon. Especially when you're doing that little dance you do while mixing batter.*

"The, uh, salmon looks good," I managed, trying to sound casual despite the butterfly convention taking place in my stomach.

"It does," Jake agreed, then laughed softly. "Though I have to admit, I'm having a hard time thinking about fish when I know I'm sitting across from the soon-to-be waffle queen of Starfall Glen. The festival's going to be something else this year."

It would be my first time participating as the official owner of the Waffle Wagon, not just as Henry Winslow's granddaughter. The festival had been a town tradition for over fifty years, and my grandfather had won the golden waffle trophy more times than anyone could count.

"Please don't jinx it," I groaned, but couldn't help grinning. "I'm nervous enough about debuting my new variation of the cheese waffle recipe." I twisted my napkin in my lap, remembering how many test batches it had taken to get the recipe just right. "Grandpa Henry always said the festival was about more than just winning. He said it was about bringing people together, sharing something special."

Jake reached across the table and gently stilled my fidgeting hands with his. "Hey, your grandfather would be proud of you, Maple. That combination of aged cheddar and herbs you came up with? It's going to blow people's minds. And I'm not just saying that because I got to be your official taste tester."

Though he definitely enjoyed that part, Pecan added. *He's remembering how you looked when you finally got the recipe right last week. All excited and covered in flour. He thought it was cute. Also, Sassy Bright was lurking around the truck yesterday, trying to figure out your secret ingredient. Want me to go mark her food truck's tires?*

I had to bite my lip to keep from laughing at Pecan's offer. Sassy Bright, owner of the Crepe Queen food truck and my main competition at the festival, had been increasingly hostile since I'd inherited the Waffle Wagon. According to Lucky, she'd been trying to get her hands on my grandfather's recipes for years.

The server appeared. We ordered. Salmon for me, steak for Jake, and I pretended not to notice when Jake quietly asked Alice to bring a small plate of bacon for Pecan.

"You know," Jake said once we were alone again, swirling his glass of red wine thoughtfully, "it's amazing how in tune you and Pecan are. Sometimes it's like he understands every word we're saying."

My hand froze halfway to my water glass. "Oh?" I tried to keep my voice light, but my mind raced. "He's just very well-trained."

Ha! As if. Remember when I ate your entire batch of test waffles last month? Or when I hid all your left shoes because you wouldn't share your bacon? Face it, Maple, I'm about as well-trained as a cat at a dog show. Speaking of which, he's remembering that time I "accidentally" knocked him into you at the park. You're welcome, by the way.

"Still," Jake continued, his eyes twinkling with something that made me nervous, "there's something special about him. About both of you, actually. I've never seen anything quite like it." He leaned forward slightly, the candlelight catching the silver at his temples. "The way you two work together in the Waffle Wagon, it's almost like..."

"Like what?" I asked, perhaps a bit too quickly.

"Like magic," he finished, observing my reaction.

I laughed, a bit too loudly, causing a couple at a nearby table to glance our way. "Special? We're about as ordinary as they come. Unless you count my grandfather's waffle recipe as something magical." I winced internally at my choice of words. "I mean, not magical-magical. Just... you know. Special. In a completely normal, non-magical way."

Smooth, Maple. Real smooth. Maybe try changing the subject before you start babbling about my collar or the time I predicted that thunderstorm by reading Mrs. Henderson's cat's mind.

Jake's smile softened. "There's nothing ordinary about you, Maple Winslow."

He's wondering if he should hold your hand again, Pecan's voice cut through my thoughts. *His palm is getting sweaty just thinking about it. Also, he's remembering how you looked last week when you were dancing around the Waffle Wagon after perfecting your recipe. He thought it was adorable. And now he's wondering if thinking about you dancing is weird. Humans make everything so complicated.*

I must have made a face, because Jake tilted his head. "Everything okay?"

"Perfect," I said quickly, taking a large sip of water. "Just, um, thinking about the festival. There's still so much to do." I wasn't entirely lying—my to-do list seemed to grow longer by the hour.

"Like what?" Jake leaned forward.

"Well, I need to finish decorating the Waffle Wagon, for one thing. Grandpa Henry always made it look so festive, and I want to do him proud." I traced the rim of my water glass. "He used to say presentation was half the battle. 'People eat with their eyes first,' he'd tell me."

Jake reached across the table again, his fingers brushing mine. "I could help with that, you know. The decorating."

"Really?" The offer surprised me, though it shouldn't have.

"Of course. I'm pretty handy with a string of lights. Plus," he added with a grin, "someone needs to make sure you don't fall off any ladders."

He's picturing catching you if you fall, Pecan commented. *Very romantic. Though personally, I think you should be more worried about Felix Montclair than falling off ladders.*

The mention of the notorious food critic in Pecan's thoughts reminded me of my other major concern. "Felix Montclair is going to be there this year," I said, voicing the worry that had been nagging at me for days.

Jake's expression darkened slightly. "The food critic? I thought he was banned from local festivals after what happened in Millbrook last summer."

"Apparently not. Lucky says he's got some kind of special invitation." I shrugged, trying to ignore the knot of anxiety in my stomach. Felix Montclair was notorious for his scathing reviews. Last summer, he'd nearly destroyed the Millbrook Farmers' Market with a series of brutal reviews that seemed more personal than professional. "I'm trying not to think about it too much."

You're thinking about it right now, Pecan pointed out. *And Jake's thinking about how he could accidentally spill something on Felix's notepad if things get ugly. I like how his mind works. Also, he's won-*

dering if he should tell you about what he overheard at the auto shop yesterday.

Before I could puzzle over Pecan's cryptic comment, our food arrived. The conversation flowed easier as we ate.

"So there I was," Jake said, gesturing with his fork, "covered in motor oil, trying to explain to Mrs. Henderson that her car wasn't making those noises because it was possessed by her late husband's spirit."

I nearly choked on my salmon. "She didn't really think that, did she?"

"Oh, she was convinced. Said George always did hate that car." Jake's eyes crinkled at the corners when he smiled. "Turned out it was just a loose timing belt."

The evening continued to unfold like a perfectly written recipe, each moment adding something special to the mix. We shared dessert, a warm apple crisp that made Pecan whine pathetically until Jake sneaked him a bite.

"Henry used to tell the best stories," Jake said, scraping the last bit of caramel sauce from our shared dessert plate. "Remember the one about the mysterious customer who paid for his waffle with a gold coin that disappeared the next day?"

I nodded, warmth spreading through my chest at the memory. "Grandpa swore it was real, but I always thought he made it up to entertain me." Now, though, with a mind-reading dog at my feet, I wondered if there hadn't been more truth to his tales than I'd realized.

Speaking of mysterious things, Pecan interjected, *Jake's thinking about asking you something important. His thoughts are all jumbled up like a basket of puppies.*

Before I could process that, Jake cleared his throat. "So, about those festival preparations tomorrow? I could come by early, maybe test a few more waffle recipes?" His attempt at casual was betrayed by the slight flush creeping up his neck.

"I'd like that," I said, and the smile that spread across his face made my heart skip.

The drive home was comfortable, with the radio playing softly in the background and Pecan sprawled across the back seat of Jake's truck. When we pulled up to my house, Jake got out to open my door. Something that made Pecan roll his eyes and mutter something about humans and their unnecessary courtship rituals.

"I had a really nice time tonight," Jake said, his voice soft in the evening quiet. The porch light caught the silver in his dark hair, and for a moment, I thought he might kiss me. He took a half step closer.

"Me too," I managed, my heart thundering in my chest. A cool breeze rustled the wind chimes Lucky had given me as a housewarming gift, their gentle tinkling the only sound besides my racing pulse.

Oh, for heaven's sake, Pecan sighed in my head. *He's thinking about kissing you, you're thinking about him kissing you, and I'm thinking about how humans make everything so complicated. Just kiss already!*

He smiled, that crooked smile that always made me feel like I was melting. "There's something magical about good company, isn't there?"

I froze. "Magical?"

"You know what I mean." He reached out and squeezed my hand gently, his palm warm against mine. "Get some rest, Maple. You've got a festival to win." His thumb traced a small circle on my palm before he let go, and the gesture sent tingles up my arm.

As I watched him walk back to his truck, Pecan pressed against my leg. *He's thinking about kissing you,* my furry friend informed me. *Also, he definitely suspects something about me. His thoughts are all swirly with questions. But mostly he's just happy you said yes to dinner. And he's already planning to bring you coffee tomorrow morning when he comes to help with the decorations.*

Chapter 2

The memory of dinner at Rosemary's Table was still fresh, making my cheeks warm as I gathered decorations from the back of Jake's truck.

"Perfect morning for setting up," he said, reaching past me to grab a box of fairy lights. His arm brushed mine. "Though I still think we could have started a little later."

He's lying through his teeth, Pecan chimed in from his perch in the truck bed. *He's actually thrilled you asked him to come early. He's been awake since five, watching YouTube videos about proper festival lighting techniques. Also, he made three different shirts try on before settling on that blue one because he remembered you said you liked it last week.*

I bit back a smile, watching Jake sort through the tangle of lights with determined focus. "Early bird gets the prime power outlet," I said, nodding toward the electrical panel near our spot.

The square was slowly coming alive with activity. Volunteers strung banners between the oak trees, their leaves hinting at autumn colors. The air hummed with excitement and the occasional clash of metal poles as booth frames took shape. The scent of fresh coffee drifted over from where The Bean Scene was setting up their stand, mingling with the morning mist.

Jake set down his box and pulled out a string of lights, holding them up to catch the early sunlight. "So, where do you want to start? I was thinking we could do something special with the awning, maybe create a sort of twinkling canopy effect."

He sketched out designs last night, Pecan informed me. *Drew little diagrams and everything. It's actually kind of adorable how much thought he's put into this. Though he's worried you'll think he's being too pushy with his ideas.*

"That sounds perfect," I said, watching Jake's face light up at my approval.

We'd just started arranging the lights when Pecan's ears perked up. *Heads up. Sassy Bright at ten o'clock, and she's already thinking about ways to peek at your recipe book. Also, she spent three hours last night practicing what she calls her 'casual festival greeting.' Spoiler alert: there's nothing casual about it.*

Sure enough, the distinctive pink-and-purple Crepe Queen food truck came rumbling around the corner, its chrome finish catching the morning light like a disco ball on wheels. Sassy parked unnecessarily close to us, her truck's side mirror nearly grazing our awning. The maneuver was so precise it had to be deliberate.

"Morning, neighbor!" Sassy called out with synthetic sweetness. She hopped down from her truck, her platinum blonde hair bouncing in a way that seemed to defy physics. Today's outfit, a pink chef's coat bedazzled with what appeared to be actual rhinestones, caught the morning light almost as dramatically as her truck. "I see you're getting an early start. Nervous about something?" Her eyes darted to the covered bowl of waffle batter I'd prepared at home.

She's wondering if that's your cheese waffle batter, Pecan reported. *Also, she's still bitter about losing to your grandfather three years in a row. And that rhinestone chef's coat? She bought it specifically to outshine your 'quaint little vintage aesthetic,' as she's thinking of it. Should I tell her vintage is actually in and bedazzling went out with flip phones?*

"Just excited," I replied, keeping my voice light as I adjusted a strand of lights. "Everything's better with a fresh start, don't you think?"

Sassy's smile tightened, creating tiny cracks in her perfect makeup. "Oh, absolutely. Especially with Felix Montclair attending this year. I heard he can make or break a business with just one review." She paused, examining her perfectly manicured nails, which, I noticed, matched her truck's color scheme. "But I'm sure you'll do fine. I mean, your grandfather's recipes are... classic."

The way she said "classic" made it sound like a polite word for "outdated." Jake must have caught it too, because he stepped closer to me, his presence steady and reassuring. The screwdriver in his hand twirled once, a nervous habit I'd noticed whenever he was annoyed.

"Speaking of classic," he said, his voice carrying that slight edge it got when he was being protective, "I think everyone's looking forward to seeing how Maple puts her own spin on things. Her cheese waffle is something special."

Oh, he's thinking about how good those test batches were, Pecan added. *Now Sassy's thoughts are turning particularly sour.*

Sassy's eyes narrowed slightly. "Is it? How interesting." She glanced between Jake and me, her expression calculating. A morning breeze ruffled the pink awning of her truck, making the gold script of "Crepe Queen" dance. "Well, I should get set up. Good luck with everything, Maple. You're going to need it."

As she clicked away in her impractical heels, which somehow didn't sink into the dewy grass, I noticed her assistant struggling with boxes of supplies, shooting pleading looks in her direction that went deliberately unnoticed.

She's already planning to send her nephew over later to "accidentally" bump into your prep table, Pecan snorted. *Want me to go leave a surprise in her truck's wheel well? Or maybe just read her recipe book's thoughts? I bet even her crepes have secrets they'd like to share.*

"Pecan," I warned under my breath, though I had to admit the offer was tempting.

Jake watched Sassy's retreat with raised eyebrows. "Well, that was subtle as a brick through a window." He turned back to me with a grin. "Come on, let's make this wagon look amazing. Show her what 'classic' really means."

We fell into an easy rhythm, working together to transform the Waffle Wagon. Jake proved to be surprisingly artistic with the fairy lights, creating elegant swoops and patterns that would look magical after dark. I focused on arranging vintage waffle irons, part of my grandfather's collection, in the display window, each one polished to a warm gleam.

He keeps stealing glances at you when you're not looking, Pecan commented as I positioned a particularly beautiful 1950s model. *Especially when you're concentrating like that. He thinks you look cute when you're focused. Also, he's wondering if it would be too forward to ask you to dinner again tonight after the festival.*

"Hey, Maple!" A familiar voice called out. Asher from The Bean Scene jogged over, his dark curls bouncing with each step, carrying a cardboard tray of coffee cups. Steam curled invitingly from the lids. "Jake asked me to bring you some fuel. Special festival blend. Extra kick for the big day."

"You guys. You're lifesavers," I said, accepting a cup gratefully. The rich aroma of his special blend, hints of caramel and cinnamon, wafted up, reminding me that I'd been too nervous to eat breakfast.

He's worried about something, Pecan observed, his tail lowering slightly. *His thoughts are all jumbled up with concerns about Felix. There's something about last summer's festival in Millbrook that's really bothering him.*

"Thanks, man," Jake said, taking his own cup. "How's the coffee booth coming along?"

Asher's usually cheerful face clouded slightly, making the freckles across his nose stand out. "It's going. Though..." He glanced around and lowered his voice. "I heard Felix already tore apart poor Mrs. Chen's dim sum stand during the setup in Millbrook last summer. Apparently, he wrote that her dumplings were 'as authentic as a plastic fortune cookie.'" He shook his head, coffee sloshing in the remaining cup. "She had to close up shop after that review went viral. Thirty years of business, gone just like that."

My stomach tightened, and not just from the coffee. I'd heard rumors about Felix's reviews, but hearing about their real impact made them more threatening.

Don't let him get to you, Pecan nudged my leg, his warm presence reassuring. *Your waffles are better than anything that pompous windbag has tasted. Though I might be biased since you always save me the crispy edges. Also, Jake is thinking about how he'd like to have a private word with Felix if he tries anything mean.*

Jake must have noticed my expression, because he touched my arm gently. "Hey," he said softly, his voice meant just for me. "Your waffles are incredible. Anyone who says different clearly doesn't know what they're talking about."

"Thanks," I managed a smile.

I busied myself with the final touches to the Waffle Wagon, arranging fresh flowers in mason jars, another of my grandfather's traditions.

Mrs. Flynn just walked by thinking about how proud your grandfather would be, Pecan commented, his tail wagging gently. *She's remembering how he used to sneak her extra waffles when she was going through her divorce. Also, she's wondering if you'll do the same cinnamon apple topping he used to make for fall festivals.*

The Waffle Wagon looked better than ever, with twinkling lights framing the service window and vintage-style bunting adding splashes of cheerful color.

"Perfect timing," Jake said, stepping back to admire our work. "Though I still think we could add more lights around the—"

He stopped mid-sentence as a hush fell over the square. The cheerful festival buzz dimmed like someone had turned down the volume on a radio.

Here comes trouble, Pecan growled softly, his fur bristling slightly. *And his thoughts are about as pleasant as week-old kibble. Actually, that's an insult to kibble.*

Felix Montclair swept through the festival grounds like a storm cloud in an expensive suit. His silver hair was perfectly coiffed, his designer glasses perched on his nose like weapons aimed at potential targets. Each step was precisely measured, his Italian leather shoes somehow avoiding every puddle and patch of grass that might mar their perfection.

He moved from booth to booth with the air of a king inspecting his subjects, making notes on his clipboard and occasionally letting out disapproving "hmms" that sent vendors into near panic.

"Is he actually wearing Italian leather shoes for a food festival?" Jake muttered, watching Felix pick his way fastidiously between puddles from the morning's setup. "That's just asking for trouble."

"Shh," I whispered, though I couldn't help smiling. The mental image of Felix slipping in a puddle improved my mood slightly.

Oh, you should hear what he's thinking, Pecan's mental voice dripped with disdain. *He's already composed three scathing reviews in his head, and he hasn't even tasted anything yet. Though... there's something else. Something about a phone call he received this morning...*

Finally, inevitably, Felix made his way to the Waffle Wagon. He looked up at my grandfather's hand-painted sign, now enhanced with my own additions, and raised one perfectly groomed eyebrow. His gaze traveled over every detail of our setup, lingering on the vintage waffle irons in a way that made me want to shield them from his judgment.

"Ah, yes. The famous Winslow waffles." His voice dripped with condescension, each word precisely chosen like ingredients in a recipe designed to intimidate. "I understand you're the granddaughter?"

He's thinking about your grandfather, Pecan's voice was tight in my head. *There's... something there. Some old history I can't quite catch. His thoughts keep skittering away from it like water on a hot griddle.*

"Yes, I'm Maple Winslow," I said, proud that my voice remained steady despite the butterflies doing acrobatics in my stomach. The morning sun caught his designer glasses, making it impossible to read his eyes.

"Hmm." He made a note on his clipboard, the scratch of his expensive pen somehow more threatening than any verbal criticism. "And I hear you're debuting a new recipe? How... ambitious." He paused, adjusting his glasses with manicured fingers. "You do realize that one word from me could make you the biggest name here. Or the biggest joke?"

Chapter 3

The threat hung in the air like the scent of burning batter. Behind me, I heard Jake shift his weight, probably fighting the urge to say something..

He's trying to intimidate you, Pecan's voice was sharp in my head. *But there's something else... he's thinking about someone else, someone who's paying him to—*

A crash from the artisanal cheese stand drew everyone's attention. The owner, still flustered from Felix's earlier inspection, had knocked over an entire display of aged cheddar. The distraction seemed to break whatever thread Pecan had been following in Felix's thoughts.

When Felix turned back to me, his smile was razor thin. "I'll be back to sample your... creation... later. Do try to make it worth my time."

He adjusted his tie, a silk number that probably cost more than my monthly rent, and turned away with surgical precision.

"Want me to accidentally spill some coffee on his clipboard?" Jake asked quietly, stepping closer. "Or maybe just his shoes? Those Italian leather beauties could use some character."

I laughed despite my nerves, the sound helping to dispel some of the tension Felix had left behind. "Don't tempt me. Though I'm pretty sure Pecan would help."

In a heartbeat, my furry friend confirmed. *I've already calculated the perfect angle to make it look like an accident. Plus, I caught him thinking about how much those shoes cost. Let's just say they're worth more than all the waffles you'll make this month.*

The morning wore on, and finally, it was time to prepare for the first round of judging. I mixed my signature cheese waffle batter with practiced movements, adding the special blend of herbs and aged cheddar that had taken weeks to perfect. Each ingredient went in with a silent prayer—not just for a favorable review, but for my grandfather's legacy.

He's coming back, Pecan warned, his mental voice tense. *And he's hungry. Actually hungry, not just professionally hungry. That's something, right? Though his thoughts are all tangled up with something else. Phone calls and meetings I can't quite make sense of.*

Felix appeared at my window just as I poured the first ladle of batter onto the iron. The sizzle and aroma of herbs filled the air. I noticed several other vendors watching anxiously from their booths, their own cooking temporarily forgotten.

The waffle iron's timer ticked away seconds that felt like hours. I could feel Jake's supportive presence behind me. Through the window, I caught glimpses of Sassy pretending not to watch while aggressively whisking crepe batter.

She's hoping you'll mess up, Pecan reported. *Though even she has to admit it smells amazing. Also, Felix's thoughts just got more interesting . He's remembering something about your grandfather, something that happened at a festival years ago.*

I worked in focused silence, letting muscle memory guide my movements as I created the perfect waffle. Each step was a dance I'd practiced countless times. The gentle lift of the iron's lid, the precise flip, the careful timing. The color was golden brown, the texture light despite the cheese, with crispy edges that would make my grandfather proud.

Felix watched every move with hawkish intensity, his pen poised over his notepad like a sword waiting to fall. When I placed the waffle before him, perfectly plated with a light dusting of fresh herbs, he pulled a syrup bottle from his pocket to top it off.

His thoughts are guarded, Pecan said, his mental voice tense. *He's intrigued, but he's... waiting for something. Or someone. I can't quite catch it. It's like he's having two conversations at once—one here with us, and one in his head with someone else. And who brings their own syrup bottle?*

The first bite seemed to take an eternity. Felix chewed thoughtfully, his expression unreadable behind his designer glasses.

A drop of morning dew fell from the awning, landing with a soft plop on Felix's immaculate sleeve. He didn't seem to notice. The aged cheddar, the blend of herbs, the perfect balance of savory and light. Everything I'd worked so hard to perfect.

Felix swallowed, dabbed his mouth with a napkin, and raised one eyebrow. The morning sun caught his glasses, turning them into mirrors that reflected my own tense expression back at me.

Maple, Pecan's voice was urgent in my head, *his thoughts just got very interesting. There's something about a phone call this morning, something about your grandfather's old recipes, and... wait... someone else is involved. Someone who's been waiting for this moment for a very long time.*

The critic's lips parted, and I felt the weight of my grandfather's legacy, my own dreams, and the entire festival's attention hanging on whatever words would come next.

Maple, something's wrong, Pecan's urgent voice cut through my anxiety. *His thoughts are scattered, jumping between pain and panic and...There's something else, something about a meeting later, but it's all tangled up with fear now.*

Before I could process Pecan's warning, Felix's face contorted. His perfectly composed expression crumpled like a failed recipe. Color drained from his cheeks before flooding back in an alarming shade of red. He reached for his water glass, his perfectly manicured fingers trembling so violently that tiny ripples formed on the surface. The glass tipped, sending water cascading across his pristine sleeve and designer tie, but he didn't seem to notice. His other hand flew to his throat, eyes widening behind those expensive frames.

"Mr. Montclair?" I stepped forward, my heart suddenly racing for an entirely different reason. The waffle iron behind me still radiated warmth, its familiar comfort now seeming somehow ominous. "Are you alright?"

He tried to speak, but only managed a strangled gasp. The sound sent chills down my spine. It was raw, desperate, nothing like his earlier cultured tones. His clipboard clattered to the ground, his precious notes scattering across the dewy grass like confetti at a funeral.

"Someone call 911!" Jake's voice cut through the growing murmurs of the crowd. He was already moving around the wagon, pushing past stunned onlookers.

His thoughts are fading, Pecan's mental voice was tight with alarm. *It's like static on an old radio, getting weaker and, wait, there's something else. Someone in the crowd is thinking about a phone call Felix received this morning. Something about threats and money, but I can't catch it clearly.*

Felix's knees buckled. He pitched forward, and only Jake's quick reflexes kept him from hitting the ground hard. Instead, Jake guided him down gently, cradling his head against the dew-dampened grass. The morning sun caught Felix's designer glasses as they slipped askew, revealing eyes that were now rolling back alarmingly.

"Is there a doctor here?" Someone shouted from the gathering crowd. "Medical personnel?"

Two festival volunteers in their bright yellow vests pushed through the crowd. One was already speaking rapidly into a radio, her voice clipped and professional. They knelt beside Felix, their movements quick and practiced, though I caught the flash of concern that passed between them.

I stood frozen in my wagon's doorway, my hands gripping the frame so tight my knuckles went white. Behind me, the waffle iron clicked as it cooled, each sound like an accusation.

The crowd is getting scared, Pecan warned, pressing against my leg. *And their thoughts are turning ugly. Mrs. Henderson is wondering if your grandfather's recipes were always safe. The cheese vendor is worried about her products being implicated. And Sassy... oh, Sassy's thoughts are particularly nasty right now. She's already composing a social media post about 'tragic accidents' and 'proper food safety.'*

The realization hit me like a splash of scalding oil. My gaze darted to the half-eaten waffle still sitting on the counter. The herbs I'd so carefully selected sprinkled across its surface like tiny warning signs I'd somehow missed. Surely it couldn't have... I'd tested the recipe dozens of times. Jake had tried it, Pecan had sampled the edges. I'd eaten it myself just this morning while doing my final preparations.

One of the medical responders looked up, her face grim beneath her festival cap. "He's not breathing. Starting CPR." The sound of their counting echoed across the suddenly silent festival grounds: "One, two, three, four..."

The medics worked with increasing urgency, their earlier professional calm giving way to tight-lipped concentration. In the distance, sirens wailed, their sound cutting through the morning. Festival-goers backed away, forming a wide circle around the scene, their phones raised like shields between themselves and what was happening.

Someone just called the health department, Pecan reported, his mental voice tense. *And the police are already on their way. Three different people made calls. The cheese vendor is panicking about her supplies being confiscated. And... Maple, there's someone at the back of the crowd whose thoughts are different. They're not shocked or scared... they're... satisfied? But they're moving away too fast for me to get a clear read.*

The crowd parted like a curtain as Detective Radcliff strode through, his badge already out. His eyes took in the scene methodically. Felix's still form, the medical responders, my wagon, and finally, me. I felt like a butterfly being pinned to a board under that gaze.

One medic stood, brushing grass from her knees. She shook her head slightly at the detective, and the gesture carried the weight of finality. Felix Montclair, the feared food critic who could make or break a business with a single review, was dead.

A collective gasp rippled through the crowd, followed by the rapid-fire clicks of phone cameras and the hurried tapping of text messages being sent.

"Miss Winslow?" Detective Rvoice was professionally neutral as he approached my wagon, but I caught the underlying edge of suspicion. "I need you to step out here, please."

Jake moved closer to me, his shoulder almost touching mine. "Maple, don't say anything without—"

"Sir," Radcliffe cut him off, his tone carrying a clear warning, "please step back. Miss Winslow, now."

My legs felt like they were made of waffle batter as I stepped down from my wagon. Pecan stayed close, his warm fur brushing against my ankle with each step. The festival grounds, which had been so full of promise just moments ago, now felt like a crime scene, which, I realized with a sickening jolt, it probably was. Oh, how does this keep happening to me?

He's already building a case in his head, Pecan warned. *His thoughts are methodical—evidence collection, witness statements, timeline reconstruction. But there's something else... he recognized Felix's name. There's some history there, something about a previous investigation that's making him extra suspicious.*

"Can you tell me exactly what happened?" Radcliffe pulled out a small notebook. His pen hovered over the paper like a bird of prey waiting to strike. Behind him, more police officers were arriving, their presence drawing even more attention from the growing crowd.

I swallowed hard, trying to keep my voice steady. "He... he was trying my new cheese waffle. He had just taken a bite, and then..." The image of Felix's face turning red flashed through my mind, making my stomach clench. "He started having trouble breathing. It happened so fast..."

"And this waffle," Radcliffe gestured to the half-eaten portion still on the counter, now being photographed by a crime scene technician, "you made it yourself? Using your own ingredients?"

"Yes, but I've tested this recipe multiple times. There's nothing in it that could—"

"Please," he held up a hand, "just answer the questions directly." He made another note, his pen scratching against the paper like fingernails on a chalkboard. "Did Mr. Montclair say anything to you before he collapsed? Any complaints about the taste or texture?"

"No, he didn't have time to—"

"Officer Thompson!" Radcliffe called to one of his colleagues who had just arrived, a younger officer whose uniform still had that fresh-pressed look. "Secure this area. No one touches anything in or around this food truck." He turned back to me, his expression unreadable but his eyes sharp. "I'm afraid we'll need to shut down your operation for now, Miss Winslow. And I strongly suggest you make yourself available for further questioning."

Chapter 4

The crowd's getting bigger, Pecan reported, pressing closer to my leg. *And their thoughts... Maple, it's not good. They're already convinced the waffle killed him. Someone's live-streaming this on social media, calling it 'Death by Waffle.' And... oh, this is interesting. Nina? She's thinking about something Felix said to her yesterday, something about exposing secrets at the festival.*

The implications of Radcliffe's words hit me hard. What should have been a cheerful morning of competition and community had become a scene from a crime drama, complete with yellow police tape now being strung around my beloved Waffle Wagon.

"Detective," Jake stepped forward despite Radcliffe's earlier warning, his protective instincts clearly overriding his usual caution. "You can't seriously think Maple had anything to do with this. She's been serving these waffles for—"

"Sir," Radcliffe's tone carried the weight of his badge, "unless you're her lawyer, I suggest you step back. This is now an active investigation."

Through the growing chaos, I could hear snippets of conversation from the crowd, each word feeling like a small cut:

"I heard he was blackmailing vendors..."

"But why would anyone use poison at a food festival?"

"My cousin ate there yesterday..."

The thoughts are even worse than what they're saying out loud, Pecan reported, his mental voice grim. *Sassy's already calling her social media manager about 'handling this crisis appropriately.' And that food blogger in the pink hat is writing a post titled 'Death at Dawn: When Food Festivals Turn Fatal.' But... wait... someone near the back of the crowd is thinking about Felix's phone records. Something about calls he made last night.*

As if on cue, I heard Sassy's voice carrying across the growing space between me and the other vendors: "I always said those old recipes needed to be properly inspected. Who knows what kind of contamination could lurk in those vintage waffle irons? Some traditions are better left in the past."

"That's enough," Radcliffe called out, silencing her with a look that could have frozen hot syrup. He turned back to me, flipping to a fresh page in his notebook. "Miss Winslow, I need you to walk me through everything you did this morning, starting with your ingredient preparation. Every detail matters."

The next twenty minutes were excruciating. Under the watchful eyes of both the police and the growing crowd, I recited my recipe and preparation methods while Radcliffe took detailed notes. Behind him, crime scene technicians in their white suits moved through my wagon like aliens investigating a crash site. They photographed everything. My equipment, my ingredients, even the vintage waffle irons my grandfather had collected over the years.

"And the cheese?" Radcliffe asked, his pen pausing. "Where did you source it?"

"From Nina's Artisanal Cheese Shop," I replied, gesturing toward Nina's booth. "She's been my supplier since I started developing this recipe. We even collaborated on the blend."

Radcliffe's eyebrows lifted slightly. "The same Nina who had a public argument with Mr. Montclair at last month's Millbrook Festival?"

The question caught me off guard. "I... I didn't know about any argument."

She did, Pecan interjected. *Nina's thoughts just went into panic mode. She's got more of a past with Felix than we know about. And... oh, this is interesting. She's not the only one he was threatening. I'm picking up scattered thoughts from at least three other vendors about similar confrontations.*

Radcliffe's eyes narrowed slightly at my response, and he made another note in his book. The scratching of his pen seemed unnaturally loud in the tense atmosphere.

"One more thing," Radcliffe said, flipping to a new page in his notebook. "Did you notice anything unusual about Mr. Montclair's behavior before he tried your waffle? Any signs of distress or illness?"

I thought back, trying to see past my own nervous anticipation of his review. The memory of Felix standing at my window seemed both recent and somehow distant. "No, he seemed... normal. Professional. Maybe a little distracted, but—"

"Distracted how?" Radcliffe's interruption was sharp, his pen poised.

"I don't know, just... checking his phone a lot. Looking around like he was waiting for someone. He kept glancing toward the festival entrance."

He's very interested in that detail, Pecan observed. *His thoughts just shifted completely.*

Radcliffe's pen paused mid-stroke. "Was he meeting someone here?"

"I don't know. He didn't say anything about a meeting."

Behind us, I could hear the crime scene technicians discussing the contents of my ingredient storage. One of them held up my specially sourced cheese blend, sealed in its branded container from Nina's shop. The sight of it made my stomach turn. What if something had been wrong with it? But no, that was impossible. I'd used the same batch in my test waffles yesterday.

"Well," Radcliffe closed his notebook with a snap that made me jump, "we'll need to run tests on everything, the remaining waffle, your ingredients, all your equipment. I suggest you make arrangements for alternative plans. This wagon won't be opening again today, possibly longer."

The words hit me like a physical blow. The Waffle Festival was supposed to be my big debut, my chance to prove I could carry on my grandfather's legacy while adding my own touch. Now it was turning into a nightmare, with police tape replacing my carefully hung bunting and crime scene photos replacing the happy customer snapshots I'd hoped to take.

Maple, Pecan's voice was urgent in my head, *something's happening over by Nina's booth. She's thinking about destroying something, some kind of paperwork. And she's not the only one acting suspicious. That sauce vendor, Mark, is packing up his supplies way too quickly, and his thoughts are all jumbled with panic about something Felix knew.*

"Detective," I tried one more time, watching as officers began cataloging my grandfather's vintage waffle iron collection, "I would never—"

"Miss Winslow," he cut me off, his tone final, "right now, all we know is that a man died immediately after eating food from your establishment. Until we determine exactly what happened, I suggest you focus less on defending yourself and more on cooperating with our investigation." He handed me his card, the edges sharp and official. "Don't leave town. We'll be in touch."

As Radcliffe walked away to consult with his team, I felt the full weight of the situation settle over me like a heavy blanket of winter snow. Around us, the festival was still technically running, but all the joy had been sucked out of the morning air. Customers who had been eagerly lining up for breakfast were now backing away, some already on their phones, no doubt spreading the news across social media.

The rumors are already starting, Pecan reported, his mental voice tinged with concern. *Someone's saying Felix had enemies at every food festival in three states. Another person is wondering if this has something to do with that health code scandal at the Millbrook Festival. And... oh, this is interesting. Lucky just arrived, and her thoughts are racing about something she sold Felix last week. Something about an old recipe book?*

Jake moved closer, his hand finding mine and squeezing gently. "We'll figure this out," he said, his voice steady despite the chaos around us.

He means it, Pecan added. *He's already thinking about calling in favors from his mechanic buddies to help investigate. Though he's also thinking about punching the next person who looks at you suspiciously, which might not be the most helpful approach. Also, he skipped breakfast and is really regretting it now that we might be here a while.*

Through the growing crowd, I spotted Nina hurriedly packing up her cheese displays, her movements jerky and nervous. Behind her booth, Mark from the sauce stand was having an intense phone conversation, his free hand gesturing wildly as he spoke in hushed tones.

"I can't believe this is happening," I whispered, watching as another officer photographed my recipe book. "Everything I've worked for, everything Grandpa built..."

Someone's recording this on their phone, Pecan warned. *And.. . Maple, there's something else. That satisfaction I felt earlier? It's back. Someone in this crowd is happy about what happened to Felix. Really happy. But there are too many thoughts overlapping for me to pinpoint who.*

My gaze drifted to where they were now covering Felix's body, preparing to move him. In the space of one bite, everything had changed. My dream of continuing my grandfather's legacy while making my own mark had transformed into a nightmare of police tape and suspicious whispers.

The sound of approaching footsteps made me turn. Lucky was making her way toward us, her usual eclectic outfit somehow subdued in the morning light. She had an expression I'd never seen before—concern mixed with a hint of guilt.

She's worried about something, Pecan reported. *Something about an antique she sold to Felix last week. She's thinking about a conversation they had, but she's actively trying not to think about the details, which is... odd.*

"Maple, dear," Lucky's voice was gentle as she reached us. "I just heard. This is terrible." She glanced around, then lowered her voice. "There's something you should know about Felix. He came to my shop last week, asking questions about your grandfather's old recipe collection. He seemed... very interested in certain details."

Before she could continue, Officer Thompson approached, his young face serious. "Miss Winslow? Detective Radcliffe needs to ask you a few more questions about your ingredient suppliers."

"Just a moment," I said to Thompson, turning back to Lucky, but she was already backing away.

"We'll talk later, dear," she called softly, disappearing into the crowd with surprising speed for someone her age.

She's hiding something, Pecan's mental voice was troubled. *Her thoughts are all tangled up with worry, but I can't make out anything specific.*

I followed Officer Thompson back to where Radcliffe waited. News crews were starting to arrive, their vans pulling up with logos blazing. A reporter from Channel 5 was already doing a stand-up near the festival entrance, gesturing dramatically toward my wagon.

"The cheese samples," Radcliffe said without preamble as I approached. "You mentioned testing the recipe yesterday. Did anyone else try it besides you and Mr. Reynolds?"

"Yes, several people. My assistant for today, Asher from The Bean Scene, Nina herself when we were developing the blend, even Mrs. Henderson from the library board." I wrapped my arms around myself, trying to stay warm despite the growing chill in my bones. "Everyone loved it. There were no issues."

Radcliffe made another note, his pen scratching against the paper. "We'll need to speak with all of them. And we'll need access to your supplier records, receipts, everything."

The crowd's getting bigger, Pecan reported. *And... Maple, someone just arrived who's thinking about documents in their car. Something that would have interested Felix. They're worried about the police find ing... wait, they're moving too far away.*

"Of course," I said, watching as more officers strung crime scene tape around my beloved wagon. The vintage sign my grandfather had hand-painted years ago, making the words "Winslow's Waffle Wagon" gleamed like a beacon. Or maybe now, a warning.

Jake stepped forward again. "I can vouch for those test batches, Detective. I was there for most of them. Everything was done by the book."

Radcliffe's eyes flickered between us. "And your relationship is...?"

"We're friends," Jake said firmly, though I caught the slight hesitation in his voice. "I help maintain her equipment, make sure everything's up to code."

He's thinking about how much more than friends he wishes you were, Pecan added.

The sound of breaking glass cut through the tension. Near Nina's booth, a jar of artisanal cheese spread had slipped from her trembling hands, shattering on the pavement. Her face was pale as she stared at the mess, but she made no move to clean it up.

"Thompson," Radcliffe called, "take her statement next. In fact, I want statements from every vendor who had contact with Mr. Montclair." He turned back to me. "Miss Winslow, I suggest you call your lawyer. We'll need you to come down to the station later today for a formal statement."

The implications of his words settled over me. This wasn't just about a ruined festival debut anymore. This was about my freedom, my future, my grandfather's legacy.

"Come on," Jake said gently, tugging at my hand. "Let's get you away from all this for a bit. We can go to my shop, figure out our next move."

As we walked away from my cordoned-off wagon, I looked back one last time. The fairy lights we'd so carefully arranged now hung limp and lifeless, their magic extinguished by the harsh reality of crime scene tape.

Don't worry, Pecan pressed against my leg reassuringly. *We'll find out what really happened. Though I have to say, for someone who just witnessed a tragedy, Sassy seems awfully interested in peeking into your recipe book while the police aren't looking.*

Someone had killed Felix Montclair. And unless I could prove it wasn't me, my life as I knew it was over.

The only question was: where do you even start investigating when you're the prime suspect, and everyone at the festival seems to be hiding something?

Chapter 5

Yellow crime scene tape fluttered in the breeze like tattered party streamers gone wrong. The cheerful bunting I'd hung now seemed to mock me, its bright colors at odds with the somber scene below.

Pecan pressed against my leg as we walked the perimeter of the festival. His presence was comforting, but made me more aware of the vendors' whispers and glances.. The usual morning bustle had taken on an almost theatrical quality, everyone trying to act normal while obviously watching my every move.

They're trying not to stare at you, Pecan reported, *but their thoughts are like a buzzing beehive of speculation. That kettle corn vendor is already planning to request a different spot next year—"away from any potential murder scenes," as she's putting it. And the coffee cart guy keeps wondering if he should dump his entire supply, just in case you touched any of his cups during setup.*

"Wonderful," I muttered, shoving my hands deeper into my pockets. "I suppose I can't blame them. Who wants to be neighbors with the Waffle Wagon of Death?"

The festival grounds, usually filled with delicious aromas, now felt tense. The cheerful chatter was gone. It reminded me of a crime scene from Grandpa's TV shows. Vendors who'd greeted me warmly just yesterday now found urgent tasks to attend to whenever I passed by.

Speaking of death, Pecan's mental voice took on an urgent tone, *Nina's heading this way, and her thoughts are more scrambled than your morning eggs. She's worried about something – several somethings, actually. And she keeps thinking about some kind of deadline.*

I looked up to see Nina approaching, and my breath caught at her appearance. The usually impeccable cheese artisan looked like she'd aged a decade overnight. Her pristine chef's coat was wrinkled and spotted with what looked like coffee stains, her dark hair escaping its neat bun in wild tendrils. She kept glancing over her shoulder, gripping her bag strap so tightly I thought it might snap.

"Maple," she called softly, her voice barely carrying over the mechanical whir of a nearby generator. "Could we... could we talk somewhere? Privately?" Her eyes darted toward a cluster of early-morning customers examining a honey display. "Please?"

I hesitated, remembering Detective Radcliffe's earlier suspicions about her connection to Felix. The way he'd zeroed in on their previous argument at the Millbrook Festival hadn't seemed random. But Nina had been more than just a supplier. She'd helped me perfect my cheese blend, spent hours testing different combinations until we found the perfect balance of sharp and creamy. She'd even shared stories about my grandfather, who'd been one of her first customers when she opened her shop.

She's genuinely scared, Pecan added, his tail lowering slightly. *And there's something about Felix she needs to tell you. But she's also thinking about some kind of payment. No, wait, that thought's gone now. She's really good at blocking certain thoughts, which is... interesting.*

"Of course," I said, gesturing toward a quiet spot between two closed booths. "Lead the way."

Nina's shoulders tensed as we walked, and she kept checking behind us with nervous energy. When we reached the relatively secluded area, she leaned against a stack of empty crates, her fingers still working at her bag strap like worry beads. "I should have told you earlier," she began, her voice barely above a whisper. The festival sounds seemed to fade away, leaving us in a bubble of tense anticipation. "About Felix. About what he... what he tried to do. What he was still doing."

"What do you mean?" I asked. The way she'd emphasized "still" sent a chill down my spine.

She glanced around once more before continuing, her fingers now moving to a thin gold chain around her neck. "Last month, at the Millbrook Festival? It wasn't just an argument like everyone thinks. He... he tried to blackmail me."

The word hung in the air between us, heavy with implications. Pecan's ears perked up, and I felt him press closer to my leg.

She's telling the truth about that part, he confirmed. *But there's more she's holding back. Something about a meeting last week. And... interesting... she keeps thinking about Lucky's shop, then forcing herself to think about cheese inventory instead.*

"Blackmail?" I repeated, trying to keep my voice steady while my mind raced through possibilities. "Over what?"

Nina's laugh was bitter. "A health code violation that never happened. He threatened to report that I was storing cheese at improper temperatures, using expired cultures. He even had photos—doctored, of course, but convincing enough to fool most people." She ran a hand through her hair, dislodging more strands from her bun. "Do you have any idea what a health code violation could do to my business? To my reputation?"

I did know. In the food industry, reputation was everything. One bad review could hurt; a health code violation could destroy. Especially for someone like Nina, whose entire business was built on trust in her handling of sensitive dairy products.

"What did you do?" I asked, watching her face carefully. Behind her, the festival was coming more fully to life.

"I called his bluff," Nina said, but her voice wavered on the last word, and her hand went back to that gold chain. "Told him I'd demand a full investigation, that I had temperature logs and security footage to prove his claims were false. He backed off, but..." She trailed off, biting her lip hard enough to leave marks.

She's thinking about money again, Pecan reported, his mental voice tense with concentration. *And something about a USB drive? The thoughts are jumbled, but there's definitely more to this story. She keeps circling back to something about a meeting at Lucky's shop, but it's like she's deliberately scrambling her own thoughts.*

"But what?" I prompted gently, noting how her eyes kept darting to the festival entrance. Early customers were trickling in.

Nina's eyes met mine, then darted away, focusing on a point somewhere over my shoulder. "But I wasn't the only one he targeted. I heard things, whispers from other vendors. Felix had a whole system worked out. Find something that could hurt someone's business, then squeeze them for whatever he could get. Sometimes it wasn't even money he wanted. Sometimes it was... information."

The implications hit me like a splash of cold water. If Felix had been blackmailing multiple vendors, that meant multiple motives for wanting him gone. My mind flashed to Mark's rushed call. Sassy's odd behavior. Lucky's cryptic warning about Felix's interest in my grandfather's recipes. A web of connections was forming, with Felix at the center like a particularly venomous spider.

"Information?" I echoed, latching onto that last word. "What kind of information?"

Her fingers twisted her necklace chain so tightly it left red marks on her skin. "Recipes. Secret suppliers. Sometimes... personal things. Things that could ruin more than just a business." She swallowed hard. "He had a way of finding out exactly what people wanted to keep hidden."

She's remembering something specific, Pecan interjected. *Something about a ledger? And there's a thought about 'The Sponsor', but she's burying it fast.*

"Did you ever hear who else he might have approached?" I asked, trying to keep my tone casual while my heart hammered against my ribs. "Any other vendors at this festival, maybe?"

Nina shook her head, but there was something too quick about the gesture, too rehearsed. "No, nothing specific. Just... rumors. You know how festivals are. Everyone talks, but nobody says anything directly." She adjusted her bag strap again, and I noticed her knuckles were white with tension.

That's not entirely true, Pecan reported, his mental voice sharp with interest. *There's so much. I can't keep up.*

"Nina," I said carefully, taking a step closer. "If there's anything else you know, anything that might help clear my name, please tell me. My entire future is at stake here. Everything my grandfather built..."

She flinched at the mention of my grandfather, guilt flickering across her face. "I'm sorry, Maple. I should have warned you about him when you told me he was judging today. I just... I wanted to put the whole thing behind me. And now..." She gestured helplessly at the crime scene tape visible from our position.

"And now my grandfather's legacy is in jeopardy because someone decided to use my waffles as their murder weapon," I finished, unable to keep the bitterness from my voice. The weight of it all, the accusations, the suspicions, the whispers, seemed to press down on my shoulders like a physical burden.

Nina's hand shot out, gripping my arm with surprising strength. "You don't think... I mean, the cheese blend we developed... I would never..." Her voice cracked, and I noticed a slight tremor in her hand.

She's panicking, Pecan observed. *But not about poison. There's something else about that cheese blend that's making her nervous. Something about... documents?*

"No," I said quickly, though doubt nagged at me. "No, of course not. We tested it thoroughly. Multiple times." I didn't add that those test batches had come from different wheels of cheese than the one used this morning.

She relaxed slightly, but her grip on her bag tightened until I could hear the leather creaking. "Right. Of course." She glanced at her watch, then started slightly. "I should get back to my booth. I have a delivery coming soon."

She's lying about the delivery, Pecan reported. *But she is meeting someone. Soon.*

"Nina," I called as she turned to leave, struck by a sudden thought. "One more thing. Did Felix ever mention anything about my grandfather's recipes? About why he was so interested in them?"

She paused mid-step, her back going rigid. For a moment, I thought she wouldn't answer. When she finally half-turned back to me, her face had gone pale beneath her makeup. "Just... be careful, Maple. Felix had a way of making enemies, but he also had powerful friends. People who might not want certain things coming to light. People who..." She stopped abruptly, pressing her lips together as if physically holding back words.

She's thinking about Lucky's shop again, Pecan reported urgently. *Something about a book. No, a collection of books. And there's that word again: 'Sponsor.'*

Before I could press further, Nina hurried away, her boots clicking rapidly against the pavement. I watched her go, weaving between booths like someone trying to avoid surveillance.

Well, that was interesting, Pecan commented, sitting down beside me. *Want to know what else I picked up while she was talking?*

"Everything," I muttered, still watching Nina's retreating form as she disappeared behind the cotton candy stand.

She was telling the truth about the blackmail attempt, but there's definitely more to that story. When you asked about other vendors, she was actively blocking thoughts about Mark and someone called 'The Sponsor.' Also, every time your grandfather came up, her guilt levels spiked.

"The Sponsor?" I repeated, the capitalization evident in Pecan's mental tone. "What's that supposed to mean?"

No idea. The thought was gone too quickly. But here's something else interesting. When she grabbed your arm about the cheese blend? She was genuinely worried, but not about poison. She was worried about something being found IN the cheese.

I frowned, trying to piece it all together. "Found in the cheese? Like what?"

Can't tell. But whatever it is, it has her spooked enough to meet with someone about it. Soon. And speaking of suspicious behavior...

I followed Pecan's gaze to Nina's booth, where she was now arranging her displays with quick, nervous movements. The morning sun caught something metallic in her hand – a key, maybe, or a USB drive like Pecan had mentioned. Whatever it was, she quickly tucked it into her pocket when a customer approached.

"So we have a victim who was blackmailing vendors," I said slowly, mentally cataloging everything we'd learned. "A cheese supplier who's hiding something about our special blend. Mysterious documents that have everyone on edge. Plus, whatever this 'Sponsor' business is about, and some kind of connection to Lucky's shop that nobody wants to talk about."

Don't forget the other vendors acting suspicious, Pecan added. *Mark's still making phone calls behind his booth, and Sassy's been watching Nina's every move since we started talking to her. Also, that new vendor – the one with the artisanal honey? She keeps thinking about some meeting Felix crashed last week.*

I sighed. "Great. So basically everyone at this festival had a reason to want Felix dead, and they all had access to my booth at some point during setup. And now it seems like my grandfather might have been involved in whatever Felix was investigating."

Look on the bright side. At least you're not short on suspects. Though I have to say, for someone who claims to have stood up to Felix's blackmail, Nina's acting an awful lot like someone who's still being threatened. Oh, and heads up. She just slipped something into that trash can by her booth. Something that made her think very loudly about Felix's last phone call.

I straightened, suddenly alert. "Really? Think we should..."

Already on it, Pecan said, trotting toward Nina's booth with the casual air of a dog simply exploring the festival grounds. I watched as he made a show of sniffing around the area, then stuck his head in the trash can when Nina turned to help a customer.

Bingo, he reported a moment later, trotting back to me. *Crumpled receipt. Nina's thoughts were practically screaming about it, something about a payment made last week. The same day Felix visited Lucky's shop, actually. And there's a phone number written on the back.*

As if on cue, Nina's phone chimed. I watched as she checked it, her face paling visibly even from this distance. She quickly packed up her display samples, hung a "Back in 15 Minutes" sign, and hurried toward the festival parking lot.

Want to follow her? Pecan asked, already alert and ready to move.

I hesitated. But Nina knew something. Something that had her scared enough to destroy evidence and run off in the middle of the busiest part of the morning. Something that might connect Felix's death to my grandfather's recipes and this mysterious "Sponsor."

"Yes," I decided, squaring my shoulders. "But carefully. The last thing I need is to give Detective Radcliffe another reason to suspect me."

Chapter 6

Following Nina would have to wait. Vendors hustled to prepare for the day ahead, but their movements held a nervous energy that hadn't been there yesterday. The usual morning chatter had been replaced by whispered conversations that died whenever anyone walked too close.

The scent of fresh coffee and warm pastries filled the air, mingling with hints of cinnamon and sugar that would normally have made my mouth water. Today, though, every smell just reminded me of Felix's last moments at my booth.

You're not the only one feeling unsettled, Pecan observed, pressing against my leg. *Everyone's thoughts are like a tangled ball of yarn this morning . All anxiety and suspicion. And speaking of suspicious...*

He directed my attention to Sassy's crepe stand, where the usually poised vendor was watching Nina's hasty departure with an intensity that made my investigative instincts tingle. I'd been so focused on Nina's odd behavior that I'd almost missed the calculating look in Sassy's eyes.

That woman's mind is more tangled than a plate of spaghetti, Pecan added, his tail twitching.

The festival grounds had taken on an almost surreal quality. Cheerful music played from hidden speakers, some peppy jazz number that seemed to mock the somber mood. Early morning customers were arriving, casting furtive glances at my Waffle Wagon. Some even crossed to the other side of the path to avoid walking near it.

A young mother pulled her child away from my booth, muttering something about "that poisoned waffle place." The words hit me like a physical blow. Was this how it would be now? My grandfather's legacy tainted by suspicion and fear?

Don't let them get to you, Pecan nudged my hand. *That woman also thinks crystals can charge her cell phone, so maybe not the best judge of character.*

I managed a small smile at that.

"Did you hear about Felix and Sassy's fight?" A voice caught my attention as I passed the kettle corn stand. Two vendors huddled behind their display, voices low but carrying just enough for me to catch snippets of their conversation. I recognized them. Carol from Kettle Corn Corner and Helen, who sold local honey and had just started doing the festival circuit this year.

"Which one?" Helen replied with a knowing laugh. She adjusted her honey display with trembling hands. "The one at the Millbrook Festival or the blow-up last week? That man collected enemies like I collect bee stings."

I slowed my pace, pretending to adjust my apron while straining to hear more. The smell of kettle corn filled the air, sweet and warm, mixing with the rich scent of Helen's honey samples.

Oh, this is getting good, Pecan reported, his ears perking up. *The kettle corn lady is remembering something about Sassy throwing a spatula. Apparently Felix dodged it, but it left a dent in Mark's sauce display. And the honey vendor. She's thinking about how Felix threatened to 'expose everything' during their argument.*

Carol leaned closer to Helen, her voice dropping even lower. "I heard she nearly lost it when he called her crepes 'glorified pancakes for the pretentious and unimaginative.' You should have seen her face. Went as red as those strawberries she uses in her filling."

"Well, you know Felix," Helen replied, arranging jars of golden honey with shaking hands. "He never could resist going for the jugular.

But Sassy's reaction was... intense. I mean, we've all had bad reviews, but the way she went after him? In front of everyone? I thought she was going to dump her entire batter bowl over his head."

"Can you blame her?" Carol glanced around before continuing. "After what he wrote about her family's restaurant in Providence? That review nearly ruined them. My cousin worked there. Said they lost half their regular customers overnight. Something about health code violations and 'questionable sourcing practices.' Never proved, of course, but the damage was done."

Helen nodded, adjusting her display again, though nothing needed fixing. "I heard he was planning another exposé. Something big. Mark from the sauce booth told me Felix was asking all sorts of questions about vendor meetings and special suppliers."

Interesting, Pecan commented. *Both of them are thinking about some kind of secret gathering.*

I exchanged a look with Pecan. This was definitely worth investigating.

"You don't think..." Carol's voice dropped even lower, "you don't think Sassy would actually..."

Helen cut her off with a sharp gesture. "Best not to speculate. Not with the police still around." She straightened suddenly, plastering on a bright smile as customers approached her booth.

Want to hear something interesting? Pecan asked as we made our way toward Sassy's crepe stand. *Every time someone mentions that argument, Sassy's thoughts get really jumbled. Like she's trying to block something out. Very suspicious, if you ask me. Also, she's been watching your booth all morning when she thinks no one's looking.*

Sassy's crepe stand was a masterpiece of French-inspired design, all delicate pastels and vintage charm. White lace bunting draped elegantly around the counter, and hand-painted signs advertised specialties like "Crêpes Suzette" and "Savory Mediterranean Delight." The whole setup usually exuded an air of effortless sophistication, but today something felt off.

The woman herself stood at her griddle, her movements precise and controlled as she spread the batter in perfect circles. But there was tension in her shoulders, a tightness around her eyes. Her usual pristine chef's coat showed signs of distraction. A small batter stain near the collar, one button fastened incorrectly.

A customer approached her booth, and I watched as Sassy's professional mask slipped into place. Her smile was perfect, practiced, but her hands trembled slightly as she poured the batter. The sizzle of it hitting the hot griddle seemed unusually loud in the morning air.

She's thinking about Felix right now, Pecan reported. *Something about a letter... no, wait, now she's aggressively thinking about chocolate sauce recipes. One tablespoon cocoa powder, two tablespoons sugar... She's really working hard to block something out. And there's something else. Every time she looks at her phone, her thoughts get really scattered.*

I waited until the customer left before approaching. "Morning, Sassy," I called, keeping my voice light and friendly. "How's business?"

She looked up, her spatula pausing mid-flip. The half-formed crepe sizzled, forgotten for a moment. "Oh, Maple. I... wasn't expecting you to be open today. After everything."

The smell of slightly burning batter filled the air as she quickly flipped the crepe. A drop of sweat rolled down her temple despite the cool morning air.

"I can't open yet until I get the go ahead from the detective," I said, noting how her fingers tightened around her spatula until her knuckles went white. "It's been quite a morning for gossip, hasn't it?"

Her laugh was a bit too sharp, a bit too quick. "People will talk about anything to avoid discussing the weather. Though I suppose a murder is more interesting than the chance of rain." She flipped another crepe with more force than necessary, making the batter splash slightly onto her pristine counter.

She's remembering something right now, Pecan interjected. *A conversation with Felix behind the festival office. Something about proof and consequences. But she's trying so hard to bury it under recipes that it's giving me a headache.*

I leaned against her counter, watching as she finished the crepe with mechanical precision. "I heard Felix could be pretty harsh with his criticism. Must be a relief, in a way, not having to worry about his reviews anymore."

The spatula clattered against the griddle, the metallic sound sharp and sudden. A few nearby customers jumped. Sassy recovered quickly, but I caught the flash of... something... in her eyes. Her hands shook slightly as she straightened the already-perfect rows of fresh fruit and chocolate sauce bottles.

"Felix was..." She paused, choosing her words carefully. "Felix had opinions. Strong ones. But he was just one critic. His words couldn't really hurt anyone who was confident in their work." She began wiping down her already-spotless counter, avoiding my eyes.

Sassy's movements became more aggressive as she attacked an invisible spot on her griddle, the cloth squeaking against the hot surface. "It wasn't just reviews with Felix," she said suddenly, her voice low and bitter. "He... he liked to dig deeper. Find things that could hurt people. Their businesses, their families, their reputations."

She's not just talking about reviews now, Pecan observed. *There's something else. And that word again. 'Sponsor.' Every time it crosses her mind, she starts reciting crepe recipes in French.*

"Must have been frustrating," I probed gently, watching her face. "Dealing with someone who had that much power over vendors' livelihoods."

Her hands stilled on the griddle. "You have no idea," she finally said, her voice barely above a whisper. "He'd show up at your booth, all smiles and charm, asking about your recipes, your suppliers. Then, just when you thought he was genuinely interested..." She trailed off, her knuckles white against the spatula handle.

"And then?" I prompted.

"Then he'd start asking different questions. About special ingredients. Private meetings. Things that weren't meant for public knowledge." She poured fresh batter onto the griddle with trembling hands. "Did you know he threatened to expose my grandmother's secret recipe? Said it violated some obscure health code. Wanted ten thousand dollars to 'forget' about it."

There's more, Pecan added urgently. *She's remembering a meeting. Lots of vendors were there. Something about protecting traditional recipes from corporate theft. Felix showed up uninvited and... oh, now she's thinking about chocolate sauce again. But whatever that meeting was about, it has her scared.*

More customers were filtering in, creating a steady stream of activity that seemed to pulse with underlying tension.

"Sounds like Felix made quite a few enemies," I said carefully, watching her reaction.

Sassy's head snapped up, eyes narrowing. For a moment, I saw real fear behind her defensive anger. "Is there something you're trying to ask me, Maple?"

I met her gaze steadily. "Just trying to understand what kind of man Felix was. Since he's the reason my business might be ruined." A customer walked past, giving us both a wide berth, and I lowered my voice. "Unless you think there might be another reason he ended up dead at my booth?"

Sassy's hand jerked, creating an imperfect circle on her usually flawless crepe.

She's thinking about last Tuesday, Pecan reported. *A confrontation with Felix. She's trying to bury the memory, but I'm getting flashes. Documents changing hands, raised voices, threats about exposure...*

"Felix," Sassy finally said, her voice tight as she scraped the ruined crepe off the griddle, "was the kind of man who thought he could make or break careers with a few well-placed words. He didn't just review food. He went after people. Their techniques, their creativity, their right to even be in this business. He'd find your weak spot and dig until you broke."

She grabbed a fresh bowl of batter, her movements sharp and angry. "What he really enjoyed was the long game. Gathering dirt, building leverage, waiting for the perfect moment to strike."

There's more, Pecan interjected. *She's remembering something specific. A review that mentioned her family's reputation. Something about traditions and shortcuts.*

"Sounds personal," I ventured, watching as she began preparing another crepe with sharp, angry movements. "I wonder what drove Felix to behave that way."

Sassy's laugh was hollow. "With Felix, everything was personal. He didn't just criticize my crepes. He questioned my family's entire legacy. Three generations of French cooking, and he dismissed it all as 'pedestrian attempts at authenticity.'" Her hands were shaking slightly as she reached for her batter bowl. "Do you have any idea what a review like that can do to a small business? Especially one built on family tradition?"

I thought about my grandfather's recipes, about the legacy he'd left me. About the Waffle Wagon and everything it represented. The morning sun caught the brass handles my grandfather had installed himself, still gleaming after all these years. "I might have some idea."

She turned back to her griddle. "But at least now the others are safe."

That's interesting phrasing, Pecan noted.

A small group of customers approached Sassy's stand, and I took that as my cue to leave.

We left Sassy to serve her customers. "Sounds like Felix had his fingers in more pies than just mine," I murmured. "Question is, who finally decided to serve him his last course?"

Speaking of suspicious behavior, Pecan started, but he was interrupted by a commotion near the festival entrance. Detective Radcliffe was back, his tall figure cutting through the crowd like a shark through water. He was heading straight for Nina's empty booth with a determined look on his face.

Oh, hold that thought, Pecan suddenly tensed beside me, his whole body going rigid. *Something's... wait... that scent... and those thoughts... they're...* His ears shot straight up, and his mental voice trailed off with an urgency.

Before I could ask what he meant, Pecan darted off between the booths, weaving through the growing crowd with surprising speed. He disappeared behind the cotton candy stand, his tail vanishing around a corner as pink wisps of sugar floated in the air behind him.

"Pecan!" I called after him, but he was already gone.

Chapter 7

I hurried after him, my shoes crunching against the gravel pathways that wound between the festival booths. The morning air was thick with competing aromas. Sweet cotton candy mixing with savory sausages, fresh coffee battling with maple syrup. My heart pounded as I tried to keep sight of my furry detective, but he'd vanished into the growing crowd.

The festival was coming to life, though there was an undercurrent of tension that made everything feel slightly off-key, like a familiar song played in the wrong tempo.

"Has anyone seen a Tibetan Terrier?" I asked, probably sounding as frazzled as I felt. A few vendors shook their heads, their expressions a mix of sympathy and suspicion. Being the owner of "that poisoned waffle place" wasn't doing much for my popularity.

Helen from the honey booth adjusted her display of golden jars and pointed toward the judges' area. "That scruffy little fellow of yours? Saw him trotting that way about two minutes ago. Seemed mighty determined about something." She hesitated, then added in a lower voice, "Though you might want to be careful over there. Detective Radcliffe's been prowling around all morning."

The judges' area was a roped-off section near the center of the festival grounds, where Felix and the other judges had been stationed yesterday. Now it stood empty, a ghost town of abandoned clip-boards and half-empty water bottles. Yellow police tape fluttered in the morning breeze, an unwelcome reminder of yesterday's events. The sight of it made my stomach clench. This was where Felix had spent his last hours, probably plotting his next round of victims before sampling my supposedly deadly waffles.

"Pecan?" I called softly, approaching the area. "Where are you, bud-dy?"

Over here! His mental voice carried a note of excitement. *Under the judge's table. You need to see this, Maple. And hurry. There's someone thinking very strongly about coming to check this area again.*

I crouched down, lifting the edge of the white tablecloth to find Pecan's nose twitching rapidly. His tail wagged with the intensity of someone who'd just discovered buried treasure.

There's something here. Something important. His nose worked overtime, sampling the air. *I can smell it. And the thoughts attached to it are... interesting. Desperate. Afraid. Angry. All mixed together like one of your experimental waffle batters.*

"What kind of thoughts?" I whispered, glancing around to make sure no one was watching. The festival crowds moved past, but no one seemed to be paying attention to the woman having a whispered conversation with her dog under a table.

Anxiety. Desperation. And... Pecan emerged from under the table, nudging me toward a pile of Felix's belongings that had been pushed to one side. Various papers and personal items were scattered about, looking like they'd been hastily searched and then abandoned. *There's something in that mess. Something that made people very, very nervous. The thoughts are practically radiating off it.*

I hesitated, eyeing the police tape. "Are you sure we should be going through his things? The police probably—"

The police aren't the ones being framed for murder, Pecan interrupted, his mental voice taking on that slightly sarcastic tone he used when he thought I was being too cautious. *Besides, they've already been through this stuff once. They missed something important. I can smell the fear all over it. And something else... something medicinal.*

He had a point. With another quick glance over my shoulder, I began carefully sorting through the pile. Most of it was what you'd expect from a food critic at a festival. Napkins with hastily scrawled notes about texture and presentation, disposable utensils, a few wadded-up wrappers bearing the names of various vendors. A small notebook filled with typical food critic observations. A festival program with certain vendors' names circled in red ink.

But underneath it all, partially hidden beneath a stack of vendor applications, I found something that made my breath catch.

A worn leather notebook, its corners softened with use, lay among the debris. The cover was unmarked except for some subtle tooling around the edges, but the pages were thick with what looked like years of notes and additions. Small pieces of paper stuck out at various angles, and colored tabs marked certain sections.

That's it, Pecan confirmed, his tail wagging faster. *That's what has everyone's thoughts in such a tangle. Every time someone thinks about it, their mind goes into overdrive. Like watching twenty different TV channels at once.*

I opened the notebook, and my eyes widened at what I found. Page after page of neat, methodical entries. Names, dates, dollar amounts. Some had check marks beside them, others angry-looking X's. The handwriting was precise, almost architectural in its clarity, suggesting someone who took pride in organization and detail. I recognized many of the names: Sassy Bright, Nina Thompson, Avery Mullen... practically every vendor at the festival was listed, along with what appeared to be their vulnerabilities and price tags.

"Oh," I breathed, flipping through the pages. The morning sun caught the edge of the notebook, illuminating tiny notes in the margins. References to health codes, supplier relationships, family histories. "He wasn't just reviewing them. He was..."

Blackmailing them, Pecan finished grimly. *I've been picking up fragments of thoughts all morning. Vendors remembering conversations with Felix, promises of payment, threats of exposure. This must be his record book. His little catalog of misery.*

The entries were meticulous, each one a carefully crafted weapon. Next to Sassy's name was a substantial figure – $10,000 – with a note about "traditional recipe violations" and "questionable ingredient sourcing." Nina's entry mentioned "health code infractions" and "supplier irregularities," along with a smaller but still significant amount. Each entry represented a potential career-ending revelation, carefully documented and priced like items in a particularly nasty catalog.

Flip to the back, Pecan suggested, his nose twitching. *There's something there. Something different. The thoughts attached to those pages feel... less angry. More sad.*

I turned to the final section of the notebook, and something caught my eye. Among the cold calculations and extortion notes, there was an entry that seemed out of place. A payment to "Dr. Wells" with a memo line that simply read "family treatment - ongoing." The amount was significant – $15,000 – and unlike the other entries, this one seemed to be money going out rather than coming in. Several following pages contained similar entries, each marked with careful notes about treatment progress and remaining payments.

That's odd, Pecan commented, his head tilting to one side. *Every other thought I've picked up about Felix has been about his cruelty, his manipulation. But that entry... it feels different. When I focus on it, I get flashes of hospital corridors and worried conversations.*

"Maybe there was more to Felix than we thought," I murmured, running my finger along the entry. "This doesn't fit with everything else we know about him. It's almost... human."

I continued scanning the pages, my stomach tightening as I realized the full scope of Felix's operation. Nearly every vendor at the festival had an entry, each with their own particular vulnerability carefully noted. Some had paid, their names marked with neat check marks.

Others, marked with X's, were presumably still holding out. The amounts varied, but they were all substantial enough to strain a small business owner's finances.

Pecan's ears suddenly perked up. *Wait... I'm picking up something. A residual thought, strong enough to leave an impression.* His nose twitched as he sniffed the notebook. *"If he pushed me any harder, I'd... I'd have no choice." The emotion attached to it is... intense. Desperate. Scared.*

I flipped to the most recent entries and found Avery Mullen's name with the largest amount yet – $25,000 – and an angry X beside it. The page corner was crumpled, as if someone had gripped it in frustration, and there were multiple crossed-out numbers, each larger than the last.

"Looks like Avery was holding out," I said softly, studying the increasingly aggressive notations. "That's a lot of money to demand from someone. And look at these notes – 'Final warning,' 'Deadline: Festival Week,' 'Full exposure pending.'"

And a lot of motivation to want Felix silenced, Pecan added, his mental voice grim. *But he's not the only one. I'm picking up so many tangled thoughts and emotions from this notebook. Fear, anger, despera tion... any one of them could have snapped. And some of these thoughts... they're not just from one person. They're overlapping, all of them afraid.*

A burst of laughter from a nearby food stand made me jump. The festival continued around us, a swirl of colors and sounds that felt increasingly surreal. How many of these smiling vendors were hiding desperate secrets? How many had been pushed to their breaking point by the man whose death I was accused of causing?

I carefully closed the notebook, my mind racing. Felix hadn't just been reviewing food. He'd been systematically destroying lives, or at least threatening to. The festival vendors weren't just competitors; they were his victims, each one potentially pushed to their breaking point. And yet, those medical payments suggested another side to him, a hidden depth that complicated the simple picture of a heartless extortionist.

"We need to keep this safe," I said, slipping the notebook into my apron pocket. The weight of it felt significant, like carrying a loaded gun. "This could be the key to proving my innocence."

And finding out who really killed Felix, Pecan agreed. *Though I have to say, the list of people who didn't want to kill him might be shorter at this point. And speaking of people...* His ears twitched. *Someone's coming. Multiple someones. And one of them is thinking very loudly about proper crime scene protocol.*

I quickly stepped away from Felix's belongings, trying to look casual as Detective Radcliffe's voice carried across the festival grounds.

The notebook felt heavy in my pocket, its secrets burning against my hip. We had evidence now—real evidence that could help solve this case.

You know what this means, right? Pecan trotted beside me as we made our strategic retreat, weaving between groups of festival-goers who were already lining up at various food stalls. *Anyone who paid Felix might have wanted to silence him to prevent future blackmail. And anyone who refused to pay might have been desperate enough to stop him from revealing their secrets.*

"Which means just about everyone at this festival had a reason to want him dead," I finished, my voice barely above a whisper. "And we don't know if we're looking for one person or..."

Or a group of very angry vendors who decided enough was enough, Pecan finished. *The thoughts I'm picking up... some of them feel connected, like shared memories. And look over there.*

I followed his subtle head tilt toward a cluster of vendors near the kettle corn stand. Nina, Sassy, and Avery stood in a tight circle, their heads bent close together in conversation. As I watched, they quickly separated, each heading in a different direction with the kind of careful casualness that screamed deliberate coordination.

Their thoughts are all tangled up with each other, Pecan observed. *Like they're all worried about the same thing, or trying to hide the same secret.*

The notebook in my pocket seemed to grow heavier. I patted it absently, feeling the worn leather through my apron. "We need to figure out who had the most to lose. Who was the most desperate." I paused. "And maybe... maybe we need to understand who Felix really was."

A young family passed by, their children clutching cotton candy and pointing excitedly at the various food stalls. The contrast between their innocent excitement and the web of darkness we'd uncovered made my heart ache. This festival was supposed to be about joy, community, and celebration. Instead, it had become a maze of secrets and suspects.

Well, Pecan's mental voice carried a note of dry humor, *at least we're not short on suspects. Though I have to say, solving a murder is a lot more complicated when you start feeling sorry for the victim. Those medical payments... they change things, don't they?*

"They do," I admitted, thinking about the careful documentation of payments to Dr. Wells. "Someone was sick. Maybe family, maybe someone close to him. Maybe Felix. It doesn't excuse what he did to these vendors, but..."

Pecan finished. *Humans are complicated. Speaking of complicate d...* His ears perked up. *Someone's watching us right now. Don't turn around, but there's a very nervous person by the lemonade stand who's thinking very hard about notebooks and secrets.*

I resisted the urge to look, instead casually adjusting my apron. "Friend or foe?"

Hard to tell. Their thoughts are like a blender full of panic right now. But one thing's clear – they know about the notebook. And they're very, very worried about what's in it. Also... He paused, his nose twitching. *They're thinking about a meeting. Something that happened last week. It didn't end well.*

In my pocket, a dead man's notebook held secrets that someone – or several someones – might kill to protect. The question was: had they already killed once? And more importantly, would they do it again to keep those secrets buried?

Chapter 8

I watched Avery Mullen from behind Helen's artisanal honey display. Golden light filtered through rows of glass jars, creating amber patterns on the dewy grass.

Under different circumstances, it might have been beautiful. But right now, my attention was fixed on Avery as he methodically arranged score sheets at the judges' station. His movements were precise and controlled, but there was something off about his demeanor. His shoulders were too tense, his movements too deliberate. Like someone trying very hard to appear normal while knowing they were being watched.

The leather-bound notebook in my apron pocket felt as heavy as a brick. Twenty-five thousand dollars. That's what Felix had been demanding from him. The kind of money that could break someone, or push them to break someone else.

Helen bustled past me, adjusting a display of lavender-infused honey. "Everything alright, dear?" she whispered, her eyes darting between me and Avery. "You've been standing there for a good ten minutes."

"Just thinking," I murmured, offering what I hoped was a reassuring smile.

He's worried about something, Pecan observed, sitting primly beside me, his fur ruffling slightly in the morning breeze. *His thoughts keep circling back to the same thing — deadlines and payments. Though I have to say, for someone who might be a murderer, he has a remarkably organized mind. Everything's filed away neat and tidy, like one of those fancy closet systems. Even his guilty thoughts are color-coded.*

Trust Pecan to find humor in even the darkest situations.

A young family walked past, their children pointing excitedly at a cotton candy machine being tested for the day. The pink wisps of sugar caught the morning light, creating an almost magical effect. But my eyes were drawn back to Avery, watching as he straightened the same stack of papers for the fourth time in ten minutes.

"Should we talk to him?" I whispered, noting how his hands trembled slightly as he worked.

Well, we could stand here all day watching him arrange and re-arrange those papers, but I don't think that's going to solve our murder problem. Besides, Pecan's tail wagged slightly, *he just thought about taking a break. Now might be our chance. And honestly, my nose is getting tired of honey. Who knew there were so many varieties?*

Sure enough, Avery was setting down his stack of papers, rubbing his temples as if fighting off a headache. His crisp blue button-down shirt looked slightly rumpled. His typically neat hair was showing signs of nervous fingers running through it. I took a deep breath, squared my shoulders, and stepped out from behind the honey display.

"Hi, Avery," I called, keeping my voice casual, though my heart was hammering against my ribs. I placed my hand over the pocket containing Felix's notebook.

He startled slightly, then tried to cover it with a quick smile. His hand jerked, knocking over a small stack of scoring cards that scattered across the table like fallen leaves. "Oh, Maple. Hi." His gaze darted briefly to the police tape still fluttering around Felix's last known location, then back to me, then to Pecan, as if he couldn't decide where to focus. "It's been quite a week, hasn't it?"

His thoughts are like a pinball machine, Pecan commented. *Bouncing from worry to worry. Felix's name keeps popping up, along with numbers. Lots of numbers.*

"That's putting it mildly." I moved closer, Pecan trotting faithfully at my heel. "I can't imagine how challenging it must be, trying to keep the judging on track with everything that's happened."

His thoughts just spiked, Pecan reported, his ears twitching forward. *The word 'judging' made him nervous. Very nervous. And there's something else... a memory of some sort. It's fuzzy, but I'm getting flashes of raised voices and slammed doors. Something about 'final warnings' and 'deadlines.'*

Avery's fingers drummed against the edge of the judges' table, creating a rapid staccato rhythm. The light caught his wedding ring as his fingers moved, and I noticed it was turned around, the stone facing his palm. A nervous habit, perhaps?

"Yes, well, someone has to maintain order, even in... difficult circumstances." He glanced at his watch, then back at me, his eyes never quite meeting mine. A bead of sweat trickled down his temple despite the cool air. "Was there something specific you needed?"

I leaned casually against the table, trying to project an air of friendly concern while my heart raced beneath my carefully composed exterior. "Actually, I wanted to talk about Felix." The drumming of his fingers stopped abruptly, leaving a sudden silence. "He had quite a reputation among the vendors, didn't he? For making people... uncomfortable."

Color drained from Avery's face, making the shadows under his eyes stand out even more prominently. A muscle twitched in his jaw, and I could see him struggling to form a response.

He's remembering something, Pecan reported, his mental voice tense. *Something about Felix's office. There's paperwork involved, an d... oh, that's interesting. A phone call he wasn't supposed to overhear. Something about payment arrangements.*

"Hey there, you two!" Jake Reynolds, his easy smile and relaxed stride a stark contrast to the tension crackling between Avery and me. He looked particularly handsome, his dark hair slightly tousled and his well-worn leather jacket.

Oh, this is interesting, Pecan's mental voice carried a note of amusement. *Jake's thinking about asking you out again, wondering if it's too soon after your last date. He's got quite the romantic streak hidden under all that engine grease.*

I felt my cheeks warm slightly, but kept my focus on Avery, who seemed to relax marginally at Jake's arrival. The change was subtle but noticeable, like someone had loosened a vice grip just slightly.

"Jake, hi. We were just discussing the... recent challenges at the festival." I watched as Avery's hands moved to gather the scattered scoring cards, his movements less precise now, almost grateful for the distraction.

Jake ran a hand through his hair, his expression sobering as he joined us at the table. He positioned himself casually between Avery and me. "It's been rough on everyone, hasn't it?" He turned to Avery with genuine sympathy. "Must be a nightmare trying to coordinate the judging now."

A group of vendors walked past, carrying boxes of supplies and chattering about their day. Their voices created a momentary bubble of normalcy, a reminder of what the festival should have been. Just another celebration of community and good food, not a murder investigation.

Avery's shoulders slumped slightly, and for a moment, he looked older than his years. The light emphasized the gray at his temples, the worry lines around his eyes. "It's... not what I expected when I agreed to judge this year." He gave a hollow laugh that seemed to catch in his throat. "To be honest, I've felt out of my depth since day one. The pressure, the politics. It's all so intense. And Felix..." He trailed off, shaking his head, his hands fidgeting with a pen he'd pulled from his pocket.

He's thinking about meetings, Pecan reported, sitting down between Jake and me. *Lots of them. Felix's face keeps popping up, but the emotions attached aren't what you'd expect from someone plotting murder. They're more... resigned. Frustrated.*

"Felix had a way of making everything more intense," Jake commented, leaning against the table next to me. His arm brushed mine slightly. "I remember last year's classic car show. He wrote this scathing review about the restoration work on Mrs. Henderson's '57 Chevy. Nearly broke her heart."

"Poor Mrs. Henderson," I murmured, remembering how the elderly woman had cried at the farmer's market for weeks afterward. The memory of her devastation felt sharper now, colored by what I knew about Felix's methods. "She'd spent her retirement savings on that restoration. Said it was her last connection to her late husband."

A shadow passed over Jake's face. "Yeah, she sold it right after that review. Couldn't bear to look at it anymore, knowing what people were saying."

Avery nodded vigorously, his pen clicking rapidly between his fingers. "That was his specialty, finding people's weak spots. He'd zero in on whatever you were most proud of, most invested in, and..." He stopped abruptly, as if catching himself.

There's something there, Pecan nudged my leg. *When he mentioned weak spots, his thoughts got all tangled up. Like he's trying very hard not to think about something specific. It's like watching someone try to hold a beach ball underwater. The harder they push, the more it wants to pop up.*

"Must have made judging with him interesting," I probed gently, trying to keep my voice casual while my heart pounded against my ribs.

"Interesting isn't the word I'd use." Avery's laugh was bitter. His fingers had stopped clicking the pen, now gripping it so tightly I worried it might snap. "Try impossible. Everything had to be done his way, scored according to his standards. And if you disagreed..." He shook his head, his fingers white-knuckled around the pen. "Let's just say he had ways of making sure people saw things his way."

"Sounds like a real piece of work," Jake said, his voice carrying an edge I rarely heard from him.

"He was." Avery's voice was quiet. His gaze drifted to the police tape fluttering in the morning breeze, then back to his papers. "But he was also... thorough. Professional, in his own way. He kept detailed records of everything."

My hand instinctively touched the notebook in my pocket, its presence suddenly burning against my hip like a hot coal. "Records?" I tried to keep my voice steady, but I could hear the slight tremor in it.

"Scores, critiques, vendor histories. Everything." Avery's eyes flickered briefly to my pocket, then away so quickly I might have imagined it. "He said it was part of being a serious critic, but sometimes it felt more like... like he was collecting ammunition."

He's thinking about a specific meeting, Pecan reported, his tail twitching with interest. *Last week, in Felix's office. There was shouting. Papers being thrown. But the strongest emotion I'm getting isn't rage or hatred. It's helplessness.*

The Avery in front of me didn't seem like a cold-blooded killer. He seemed like a man caught in a web he couldn't escape, like everyone else listed in Felix's notebook.

Jake, to ease the tension, steered the conversation toward safer waters. "Hey, speaking of records, Maple, did I tell you about the vintage radio I'm restoring? It's from the '40s, absolutely beautiful piece. Found it at that estate sale over on State Street."

"The Walker estate?" Avery asked, visibly relieving at the change of topic. Some color returned to his face, and his death grip on the pen loosened slightly. "I heard they had quite a collection."

"You should see it," Jake continued, his eyes lighting up with genuine enthusiasm. "All original parts, even the vacuum tubes. Though getting the frequency selector unstuck has been a real challenge. Had to fabricate a replacement spring because they don't make them any more..."

As Jake chatted, I watched Avery's posture gradually relax. His death grip on the pen loosened, and color returned to his face. He even smiled genuinely once or twice, especially when Jake described his ongoing battle with a particularly stubborn carburetor. It was hard to reconcile this version of Avery. The one who laughed at Jake's mechanical mishaps and offered surprisingly knowledgeable comments about classic cars with the desperate man who might have murdered Felix.

Humans are like puzzles, Pecan observed sagely, watching a butterfly land briefly on a nearby flower.

The conversation wound down naturally, and Avery checked his watch again. "I should get back to it. These scores won't tabulate themselves." He gathered his papers with steadier hands than before, then paused, looking at me with an expression I couldn't quite read. Something that might have been regret. "Maple... I hope they figure out what really happened to Felix. For everyone's sake."

I nodded, watching him walk away. His shoulders had straightened somewhat, but there was still a weight to his steps.

Jake touched my arm gently, his hand warm and steady against my skin. "You okay? You looked like you just saw a ghost."

I forced a smile. "Just thinking." I glanced at him, suddenly very aware of his proximity and the concern in his eyes. "Thanks for jumping in back there. The conversation was getting a bit..."

"Intense?" He grinned, his thumb absently rubbing small circles on my arm. "Yeah, I noticed. You looked like you were about to go full detective mode on poor Avery."

"Was I that obvious?"

"Only to someone who knows you," he said. "Listen, I was wond ering..."

Oh, here it comes, Pecan's mental voice was practically gleeful. *He's going to ask you out again. His thoughts are practically doing cartwheels.*

But before Jake could finish his sentence, a commotion erupted from the direction of the parking lot. Raised voices carried across the festival grounds, cutting through the morning air like a knife. Both of us turned to look, the moment shattered.

CHAPTER 9

The shouts from the parking lot sliced through the peaceful morning like a knife through butter. Jake and I exchanged glances before hurrying toward the commotion, our footsteps crunching against the gravel. Pecan trotted alongside us, his ears perked forward and tail held high with curiosity.

Oh my, Pecan's mental voice carried a note of excitement. *There's enough angry thoughts flying around over there to fill one of your grandfather's recipe books. And some of them are quite creative in their use of colorful language.*

Through gaps in the gathering crowd, I caught glimpses of Mark, the artisanal sauce vendor, facing off against a burly man in a delivery uniform. Mark's usually pristine appearance was distinctly ruffled – his carefully styled dark hair stuck up at odd angles as if he'd been running his hands through it repeatedly, and his crisp white apron was askew. His face had turned an alarming shade of red that nearly matched his signature hot sauce.

"This is highway robbery!" Mark's voice cracked with emotion, the sound carrying across the parking lot. Several early-morning festival-goers paused their setup to watch the unfolding drama. "We had an agreement on pricing! You can't just change the terms whenever you feel like it!"

The delivery man, his name tag identified him as "Steve", remained unmoved, his clipboard held like a shield between them. He had the weary expression of someone who'd had this conversation too many times before. "Prices change, Mark. You know how business works. But that's not even the real issue here, is it?" He waved the clipboard with a sharp gesture. "You're three payments behind. Three!"

His thoughts are absolutely everywhere, Pecan reported, settling into a sitting position beside me. *Like one of those pinball machines at Jake's garage, bouncing from money troubles to recipe alterations to... oh, interesting. There's something about Felix in there, all mixed up with numbers and threats. And my, my... quite a vivid fantasy about dumping an entire vat of ghost pepper sauce into someone's morning coffee.*

I edged closer, trying to blend in with the growing crowd. All attention was focused on the unfolding confrontation.

"You don't understand," Mark's voice dropped to a desperate hiss, his hands gesturing wildly. "I had unexpected expenses. Things happened that were beyond my control—"

"Beyond your control?" Steve barked out a laugh that held no humor. "Like what? That fancy new packaging you didn't need? Or maybe it was all those 'consulting fees' you kept complaining about?" He jabbed a thick finger at the clipboard. "The numbers don't lie, Mark."

Mark flinched as if he'd been physically struck. His hands clenched into fists at his sides, and I could see his knuckles turning white with tension. A muscle twitched in his jaw, and for a heart-stopping moment, I thought he might actually take a swing at Steve.

Whoa, Pecan's mental voice was sharp with surprise. *That really hit a nerve. When Steve mentioned consulting fees, Mark's thoughts went straight to Felix. There's a memory... clear as day. Felix sitting in Mark's shop, sampling sauces and making demands. Something about 'protecting your reputation' and 'reasonable compensation.' And there's more... something about recipe changes and threats.*

The crowd had grown larger, forming a loose circle around the two men. Nina watched with particular interest, her arms crossed tightly over her chest. I remembered Felix's notebook. How many of these people had their own stories of his manipulation?

Jake stepped forward, his movement smooth and purposeful. He had a way of commanding attention without seeming to try, and even now, dressed in his work clothes, he projected an air of quiet authority.

"Hey folks," his voice carried easily across the tension-filled space. "Maybe we could take this somewhere more private? No need to air all this out in the parking lot."

He positioned himself slightly between Mark and Steve, not quite interfering but definitely creating a buffer zone. The morning sun caught his dark hair, highlighting threads of auburn I'd never noticed before. Focus, Maple, I chided myself. This wasn't the time to get distracted by Jake's... everything.

"Stay out of this, Reynolds," Mark snapped, but there was a tremor in his voice that betrayed his gratitude for the intervention.

Steve jabbed the clipboard toward Mark again, the papers rattling with the force of his gesture. "Private? Like how you've been privately ducking my calls for weeks? Or privately promising payment 'any day now'? I've got a business to run too, you know!"

"I told you, after Felix—" Mark cut himself off abruptly, his face draining of color so quickly I worried he might faint. The name hung in the air like smoke, heavy and acrid.

I warned Felix not to mess with me, Pecan relayed, his tail twitching with interest. *That's what he just thought. Clear as a bell.*

My heart skipped a beat. I reached down to scratch behind Pecan's ears, trying to appear casual while my mind raced. What exactly had Felix done to Mark? And more importantly, what had Mark done about it?

A festival security officer finally pushed through the crowd, his yellow vest almost painfully bright in the light. He was young, probably new to the job, but he carried himself with practiced authority. "What seems to be the problem here?"

"No problem," Mark said quickly, too quickly. His hands fluttered nervously at his sides like trapped birds. "Just a minor business disagreement. Everything's fine."

Steve snorted, the sound sharp with disbelief. "Minor? Three missed payments isn't minor, Mark. And let's talk about these invoices you've been disputing—"

"I had to dispute them!" Mark's composure cracked, his voice rising to a near-shout. "After everything that happened with that damn critic, what choice did I have? He ruined everything!"

The crowd collectively inhaled, and I felt the shift in the air. The way everyone seemed to lean forward slightly, hungry for details about

Felix's latest transgression. Even in death, he was still stirring up trouble.

His thoughts just went into overdrive, Pecan reported, pressing closer to my leg. *Felix was pressuring him to alter his signature sauce, threatening to expose something if he didn't comply.*

Jake stepped closer to Mark, his voice low and steady, carrying that natural calm that seemed to follow him everywhere. "Hey, man, take a breath. Whatever's going on, this isn't the way to handle it." He glanced meaningfully at the growing crowd of onlookers, some of whom had their phones out, recording the scene.

The security officer nodded in agreement, adjusting his yellow vest with nervous authority. "If you folks can't resolve this civilly, you'll need to leave the festival grounds. We can't have this kind of disruption."

"Fine," Steve tucked the clipboard under his arm with a sharp movement. "But this isn't over, Mark. You've got until the end of the week to sort this out, or we're terminating our contract. No more extensions, no more excuses."

As Steve turned to leave, Mark's shoulders slumped like a puppet with cut strings. "You don't understand," he muttered, more to himself than anyone else. "None of you understand what he did. What he made me do."

The crowd dispersed, drifting back to their routines, but I lingered, watching Mark gather himself. His hands shook slightly as he straightened his apron, the movement almost compulsive. I remembered how proud he'd been when he'd first started at the festival three years ago.

There's more, Pecan's mental voice was thoughtful, his ears twitching as he caught fragments of Mark's thoughts. *He's thinking about papers, documents of some kind. And... wait... 'No one will find out the rest... if I can keep my story straight.'*

What story was Mark trying to keep straight? And what else was he hiding behind that carefully cultivated image of an artisanal sauce maker?

"You okay?" Jake's voice was soft beside me.

"Just thinking," I replied, watching as Mark retreated to his vendor stall, his movements stiff and mechanical. "There's something not right about all this."

"With Mark?" Jake said. "Yeah, I got that feeling, too. He's usually so... controlled. I've never seen him lose it like that."

Oh, he's worried about you, Pecan chimed in, his tail wagging slightly. *He's thinking about how you always find trouble, and how he wishes he could help more.*

Before I could respond, to Jake or Pecan, a familiar voice cut through the air like a cold wind.

"Miss Winslow." Detective Radcliffe's voice carried that particular tone that meant trouble. I turned to find him standing a few feet away, his expression unreadable beneath his perpetual five o'clock shadow. "A word?"

Jake touched my arm lightly, his fingers warm through my sleeve. "Want me to stick around?"

I shook my head, trying to project confidence. "I've got this. Thanks." I managed a smile that I hoped looked more assured than it felt. "Rain check on that conversation we almost had earlier?"

His answering smile was warm. "Count on it."

I followed Detective Radcliffe away from the dispersing crowd. Pecan trotted beside me.

Detective Radcliffe led me toward a quiet corner of the parking lot, where festival banners snapped in the breeze like restless flags. The sound of the crowd faded behind us, replaced by the soft crunch of gravel under our feet and the distant hum of traffic. He stopped near a row of empty vendor spaces. His expression was even harder to read than usual.

"Quite a show back there," Radcliffe commented, his tone carefully neutral. He stood with his hands in his pockets, but I noticed how his right hand kept twitching slightly, as if reaching for his notebook.

"Just a business dispute," I said, aiming for casual, but probably missing by a mile.

He's thinking about Mark's outburst, Pecan reported, sitting primly between us. *Specifically, about the Felix connection. But there's something else... he's got new information. Something that's making him reconsider his initial theories. And... oh, interesting. He's been looking into Felix's bank records.*

Radcliffe's eyes narrowed slightly, reminding me of a hawk spotting movement in the grass. "Funny how Felix Montclair's name keeps coming up in these 'business disputes,' isn't it? Almost like he had his fingers in everyone's pies... or, in this case, sauces."

I met his gaze steadily, though my heart was doing an impressive gymnastics routine in my chest. "Felix seems to have had that effect on people."

"So I'm learning." Radcliffe finally pulled out his notebook – a standard-issue police notepad. "In fact, I've been learning quite a lot about our deceased critic lately. Care to guess what kind of interesting patterns are emerging?"

I waited until a group passed by before responding. "I imagine there are quite a few people who weren't fans of his work."

Radcliffe's pen tapped against his notepad in a steady rhythm that seemed designed to get under my skin. "That's putting it mildly. But what's really interesting is how many of those people are right here at this festival. Mark, for instance." He gestured vaguely toward where the confrontation had taken place. "Did you know Felix wrote a scathing review of his sauces last year? Called them 'amateur attempts at culinary relevance' and questioned the authenticity of his family recipes."

I hadn't known that specific detail, but it fit the pattern emerging from Felix's notebook perfectly. "That must have hurt his business."

"Oh, it did more than hurt." Radcliffe's pen stopped tapping, and the sudden silence felt loaded with meaning. "It nearly destroyed it. Mark's sales dropped by sixty percent after that review. He had to take out loans just to keep his shop open." He paused, watching my reaction with those sharp eyes. "But then, mysteriously, Felix wrote a follow-up review six months later, praising Mark's 'improved' recipes and 'newfound sophistication.'"

Detective Radcliffe's thinking about bank records, Pecan interjected. *There were unusual payments from Mark's accounts around the time of that second review. And... oh! He's got a whole timeline mapped out in his head. Felix's positive reviews seem to correlate with large cash withdrawals from various vendors' accounts.*

The implications were clear as crystal. Felix had used his influence to force Mark to change his recipes, probably while extracting "consulting fees" in the process. Just like he'd done with so many others listed in that damning notebook.

"Sounds like Felix had a particular way of doing business," I said carefully.

Radcliffe's laugh was short and humorless, more of a bark than actual amusement. "That's one way to put it. Another way would be systematic extortion." He flipped through his notebook with deliberate slowness. "We've been following the money, Ms. Winslow. And let me tell you, it leads to some very interesting places."

A gust of wind caught the festival banners, making them snap sharply against their poles.

"Why are you telling me this?" I asked finally, when the silence had stretched too thin.

He closed his notebook with deliberate slowness. "Because I think you already know more than you're letting on. And because I'm starting to wonder if Felix's death wasn't just about your waffles after all."

Before I could respond, a sharp whistle cut through the air like a knife. We both turned to see Officer Chen waving urgently from across the parking lot, her expression suggesting something required immediate attention.

Chapter 10

Detective Radcliffe strode away with Officer Chen, leaving me standing in the parking lot with my thoughts spinning like a waffle in a broken iron. Pecan huffed.

He's worried about you, Pecan's mental voice was gentle. *And there's something else... something about evidence they found in Felix's hotel room.*

I needed to find Jake. With each passing minute, the information inside Felix's notebook seemed more dangerous than a vat of boiling oil.

A group of teenagers nearly bowled me over in their rush to get to the cotton candy stand, reminding me that I needed to keep moving. Standing still made me feel like a target, and after Radcliffe's cryptic warnings, that was the last thing I needed.

Jake's over by the maintenance shed, Pecan offered, dodging a runaway stroller. *And he's not alone. Mark's with him. Their thoughts are... intense. Lots of worry about money and reputation.*

I wound my way through the growing crowd, sidestepping a woman trying to wrangle three small children while balancing a precarious stack of funnel cakes. The giant waffle mascot, someone in a foam costume that had seen better days, was taking selfies with visitors, its permanent plastic smile somehow looking slightly maniacal.

As I approached the maintenance shed, the low murmur of voices carried on the breeze. Jake stood with his back against the weathered wood, arms crossed, listening intently to Mark, who was gesturing animatedly. Mark's earlier dishevelment hadn't improved. If anything, he looked more frazzled, like a man watching his carefully constructed world unravel thread by thread.

"—just don't know what I'm going to do," Mark was saying, his earlier composure still notably absent. "If I lose my supplier, everything's finished. You don't understand, Jake. This isn't just about the festival. My whole business—" He wrung his hands. "The timing couldn't be worse. With Felix gone, and now this..."

Jake caught sight of me and straightened, relief washing over his features. "Maple."

Mark's head snapped around, his expression shifting from desperation to wariness in an instant. "I should go," he muttered, already backing away. "Got to get my booth ready. The rush—"

He's thinking about Felix again, Pecan reported, ears perked forward with interest. *And something about recipes in a safe.*

"Mark," I called after him, but he was already disappearing into the crowd.

Jake pushed away from the shed wall, closing the distance between us. "You okay? What did Radcliffe want? You look like someone just told you they're banning waffles from the state."

I glanced around, noting the steady stream of people passing nearby. A couple of teenage girls were watching Jake with poorly concealed interest, giggling behind their phones. "Not here. Is there somewhere quieter we can talk?"

He nodded, understanding immediately. That was one of the things I appreciated most about Jake, his ability to read a situation without needing every detail spelled out. "Follow me."

He led us behind the maintenance shed to a small clearing bordered by oak trees that must have been there since before the festival grounds existed. Festival sounds drifted over, muted by distance and foliage, creating a pocket of relative peace. A wooden bench, weathered but solid, sat beneath the largest oak, probably a refuge for tired maintenance workers needing a moment's escape.

"This should work," Jake said, settling onto the bench. The wood creaked softly under his weight. "Now, what's going on? You've got that look you get when you're about to tell me something that's going to complicate both our lives."

I sat beside him, Pecan positioning himself as a furry sentinel, his tail swishing against the grass. The notebook seemed to burn in my pocket as I pulled it out.

"I found something in Felix's belongings," I said, keeping my voice low despite our relative privacy. "Something that might explain why so many people wanted him dead."

Jake's eyebrows rose as I handed him the notebook. The leather cover was worn smooth from handling, and several pages stuck out at odd angles. He flipped it open, his expression growing more serious with each page turn.

"These are all festival vendors," he said slowly, his finger tracing down one particularly full page. "And these numbers... are these payment amounts?"

"I think so." I leaned closer, our shoulders touching as I pointed to specific entries. "Look at the dates. They correspond with when Felix published reviews, both negative and positive ones. See here?" I indicated a particularly damning entry. "Nina's cheese shop. Negative review in March, followed by a mysteriously glowing review in April, right after this payment."

Someone's coming, Pecan warned. I straightened quickly as a maintenance worker walked past, pushing a cart of supplies that squeaked in desperate need of WD-40. We waited until they were well out of earshot before continuing.

"So Felix was what? Blackmailing vendors? That's..." He shook his head, disgust in his expression. "Actually, knowing what we do about Felix, that's not even surprising."

"It looks that way. He'd write a scathing review, then offer to 'reconsider' his opinion for a price." I tapped the page where Mark's name appeared, the ink slightly smudged as if written in haste. "That's probably what that confrontation was about earlier. The 'consulting fees' his supplier mentioned? I bet Mark was struggling to pay both Felix and his regular bills."

"Makes sense." Jake frowned at a particular entry, his forehead creasing in concentration. "What do you make of these medical notes? They seem out of place in what's otherwise basically a blackmail ledger."

I leaned in again. The entry he indicated was different from the others. No payment amounts, just cryptic references to treatment schedules. The handwriting was shakier too, less confident than Felix's usual precise script.

Maple, Pecan's mental voice carried an edge of urgency that made my spine stiffen. *Detective Radcliffe is heading this way. And his thou ghts... they're not good. There's something about evidence and warrants, and he's rehearsing your rights in his head.*

Before I could process this warning, Radcliffe's voice cut through our secluded spot like a blade through butter. "Ms. Winslow."

Jake and I jerked apart like guilty teenagers. I slipped the notebook into his jacket pocket as we stood, the movement hidden by our bodies. Radcliffe emerged from between the trees, his expression grim. Officer Chen flanked him, his hand resting near his weapon in a way that made my stomach clench.

"Detective," I said, aiming for casual, but probably landing somewhere between nervous and guilty. "What brings you out here? The festival's best attractions are in the other direction. Though I suppose you're not here for the deep-fried cookie dough."

"New evidence has come to light." Radcliffe's voice was flat, professional, with an undercurrent of satisfaction that made my blood run cold. "We found a draft of Felix's review of your waffles in his hotel room. It wasn't favorable."

My stomach dropped. "What?"

"In fact," Radcliffe continued, pulling out a folded paper from his jacket, "he planned to publish a review that would have effectively destroyed your business. Called your waffles 'an insult to the culinary arts' and suggested your grandfather would be 'spinning in his grave at what his beloved recipe had become.' Quite a motive for murder, wouldn't you say?"

Jake stepped forward, his protective instincts kicking in like a well-oiled machine. "That's ridiculous. Maple would never—"

"Mr. Reynolds," Radcliffe cut him off, "unless you want to be charged with interfering with a police investigation, I suggest you step back. This doesn't concern you."

He's serious, Maple, Pecan's mental voice was tight with worry. *They found traces of something in Felix's system. And... oh no. There's surveillance footage they're using as evidence. Something about you arguing with Felix before he died.*

"Maple Winslow," Radcliffe's voice took on the formal tone I'd heard too many times on TV shows, but never expected to hear directed at me, "you're under arrest for the murder of Felix Montclair. You have the right to remain silent. Anything you say can and will be used against you in a court of law..."

The words washed over me like cold syrup, sticky and suffocating. I saw Jake's face contort with protest, saw Officer Chen move to block him. Pecan pressed against my legs, whimpering in a way that broke my heart.

This isn't right, Pecan's thoughts were frantic. *The real killer is still out there, and Detective Radcliffe's thoughts are all focused on the wrong evidence. He's not even considering the other suspects!*

"Jake," I managed, my voice surprisingly steady despite the earthquake happening in my chest. "Take care of Pecan for me?" Our eyes met, and I tried to convey everything I couldn't say aloud. The notebook. The investigation. The trust I was placing in him. The way my heart seemed to stutter every time he looked at me like that.

He nodded, jaw tight enough to crack walnuts. "I'll figure this out, Maple. I promise." His hand unconsciously patted his jacket pocket where Felix's notebook lay hidden, and I saw the determination settle over his features.

Radcliffe produced handcuffs, the metal catching the sun in a way that seemed almost mocking. He secured them around my wrists. Not too tight, but tight enough to remind me this wasn't some bizarre dream. I caught one last glimpse of Jake and Pecan. My friend and my magical companion, standing together beneath the oak trees like guardians in a fairy tale gone wrong.

"Let's go," Radcliffe said, guiding me away from the clearing with a firm hand on my elbow.

Don't worry, Maple, Pecan's mental voice followed me, strong and clear despite the growing distance. *Jake's already thinking about the notebook. And I'll help him. We won't stop until we find the truth.*

As Radcliffe led me through the festival grounds, past shocked vendors and curious onlookers, I held onto that thought like a lifeline. And now Jake had the key to unraveling it all, assuming he could decode Felix's notes before it was too late.

We passed Mark's sauce booth, where he stood frozen, a bottle of hot sauce suspended mid-air as he watched my walk of shame. His face drained of color when our eyes met, and I saw him quickly turn away, knocking over a display in his haste.

His thoughts are chaos, Pecan reported from somewhere behind me. *Guilt, relief, and... fear. So much fear, Maple.*

"Watch your head," Radcliffe instructed as he helped me into the back of the police car. The seat was cold and hard.

Through the window, I could see the festival continuing, as if one of its vendors hadn't just been arrested for murder. The giant waffle mascot was still taking pictures, children were still running between booths, and somewhere in that crowd, a killer was watching me being taken away.

The last thing I saw before Radcliffe closed the door was Jake kneeling beside Pecan, one hand on my dog's head while the other clutched his jacket pocket. He looked up, caught my eye, and gave me a slight nod.

As the police car pulled away from the festival grounds, Pecan's thoughts reached me one last time before we turned the corner. *Stay strong, Maple. We'll find the truth. And when we do, someone's going to learn that messing with the Waffle Wagon family was their biggest mistake.*

After what felt like years but was probably only hours, Officer Chen appeared with his keys jingling.

"Your bail's been posted, Ms. Winslow."

I found Jake and Pecan waiting in the lobby, my furry friend's tail wagging so hard his whole body wiggled. Jake looked tired but relieved, his usual easy smile strained around the edges.

"Let's get out of here," he said.

Detective Radcliffe's voice followed us out. "Don't leave town, Ms. Winslow. This isn't over."

Jake's truck sat in the parking lot, and Pecan immediately jumped into the middle seat as if he'd been riding there his whole life. I slid in after him.

Once we were on the road, Jake pulled Felix's notebook from his jacket pocket. "I've been thinking about this. Maybe we should turn it over to Radcliffe."

Bad idea, Pecan chimed in. *The detective's already convinced he has his killer. He'll just file it away as irrelevant.*

I took the notebook and ran my fingers over its worn cover. "Radcliffe's not looking for other suspects. But this notebook? It's full of them. Look at all these people Felix was blackmailing. They all had motives."

Jake drummed his fingers on the steering wheel. "It's risky, Maple. Keeping evidence from the police..."

"I know." I sighed, watching the streetlights blur past. "We'll give it to them, eventually. But first, we need to figure out what these medical notes mean, and why Felix was keeping track of them. There's something here we're missing."

"Alright," Jake said after a moment. "But we do this carefully."

I opened the notebook, studying the names listed there.

Jake pulled into my driveway, but left the engine running. "Why don't you get some sleep and we'll attack this fresh tomorrow morning?"

I nodded and stepped out of the truck.

You know, Pecan's mental voice had that tone he got when he was trying to be casual but actually had something important to say, *before Jake comes tomorrow, you could try your scrying.*

He had a point. I needed every advantage I could get.

CHAPTER 11

Sleep had eluded me most of the night. The hours had crawled by, marked only by Pecan's occasional dream-induced whimpers. Every time I closed my eyes, I saw Detective Radcliffe's satisfied expression as he'd snapped those handcuffs around my wrists.

By dawn, I'd given up on rest entirely and found myself in my kitchen, measuring flour with the precise movements Grandpa Henry had drilled into me since childhood. One cup, level exactly with the back of a knife. Two cups. Three. The familiar motions were soothing, even if my purpose this morning wasn't exactly culinary.

The kitchen was quiet except for the soft clink of measuring cups and the occasional whine of early morning wind against the windows. The neighbor's rooster, an annoying but reliable alarm clock, had just begun his morning performance.

You're doing the right thing, Pecan's drowsy thoughts drifted from his cushion in the corner, where he'd curled himself into a perfect cinnamon roll shape. *Though I still think the whole 'seeing visions in waffle batter' thing is weird, even for someone with a talking dog. And I should know—I'm the talking dog. Also, you're measuring that flour too carefully. It's scrying, not the state fair competition.*

"Says the telepathic terrier," I muttered, cracking eggs into my mixing bowl with perhaps more force than necessary. A bit of shell fell in, and I fished it out with trembling fingers. As I reached for the vanilla extract, I forced them steady. I couldn't afford mistakes. Not with scrying, and certainly not with a murder investigation hanging over my head.

The vanilla scent wafted up, reminding me of countless mornings spent in this kitchen with Grandpa. He'd always said vanilla was more than just flavoring. It was a bridge between worlds, a catalyst for magic. At the time, I'd thought he was being poetic. Now, watching the amber drops ripple through my batter, I wondered what else he'd tried to teach me that I'd missed.

Detective Radcliffe's evidence is circumstantial at best, Pecan offered, stretching and padding over to sit at my feet. His fur brushed against my ankle. *That surveillance footage only shows you arguing with Felix, not killing him. And honestly, who hasn't wanted to argue with that pompous pastry critic? I once heard him say dogs shouldn't be allowed near food trucks. The nerve!*

I furiously whisked the batter, watching the ingredients blend. "Which is exactly why we need to figure out where else Felix went that day. Someone poisoned him, and it wasn't in my waffles." I paused, adding a pinch of cinnamon, Grandpa's secret ingredient. "Though I have to admit, the list of people who wanted to poison him seems to grow by the minute."

The notebook Jake has certainly proves that, Pecan agreed, his tail swishing against the kitchen tiles. *All those vendors Felix was black mailing... it's like a murder mystery dinner theater, except with more waffles and less terrible acting.*

The batter smoothed under my whisk, becoming glossy and perfect. But instead of pouring it into the waffle iron, I set the bowl on my counter and took a deep breath. Scrying wasn't exactly my strong suit. I had only recently learned about this ability, and I had no idea how to refine it to be effective in providing me answers.

"The answers we seek often hide in the familiar, maple sugar," Grandpa had told me once, his weathered hands steady as he poured batter into his beloved waffle iron. "Some folks look to fancy tools and complicated methods, but us Winslows? We've always found our truth in the simple things we know and love." At the time, I'd rolled my eyes at what I thought was just another of his cryptic kitchen philosophies. Now, standing in my kitchen with murder accusations hanging over my head, those words felt like a lifeline.

I placed my hands on either side of the bowl and closed my eyes, focusing on Felix's last day at the festival. The ceramic was cool beneath my palms, but the batter itself grew warm, almost humming with energy. A tingling sensation crept up my arms, like static electricity but gentler, more purposeful.

Your hands are glowing, Pecan observed, his mental voice a whisper tinged with fascination. *Just a little, around the edges.*

When I opened my eyes, the surface of the batter had become mirror-smooth, reflecting something that wasn't my kitchen ceiling. The transformation was subtle but unmistakable. The creamy surface now had an otherworldly sheen, like mother-of-pearl in moonlight.

Images formed in the creamy surface: the festival grounds, early morning sunshine casting long shadows across empty paths. I saw Felix's distinctive figure moving between booths, his notebook in hand. His movements were purposeful, predatory almost, as he made his rounds. He paused at several vendors, but one spot held his attention longer than the others.

The vision was frustratingly unclear, like trying to watch television through static, but I could make out a booth near the eastern edge of the festival grounds. Something about the angle of Felix's shoulders suggested tension, maybe even fear. He wrote something in his notebook, something that made his hands shake.

I leaned closer, trying to make out more details. The booth's banner fluttered in the vision's breeze, almost readable. There was something about the colors, something familiar...

Someone's coming, Pecan's warning broke through my concentration like a splash of cold water. *It's Jake. And Lucky's with him. And Jake's thinking about that notebook. He's been up all night trying to make sense of it. Also, Lucky's wearing something that smells like lavender and... is that sage?*

The images in the batter dissolved instantly, leaving me staring at ordinary waffle mix. I barely had time to slide the bowl aside before a knock echoed through my house, making me jump despite Pecan's warning. My heart hammered against my ribs.

"Maple?" Jake's voice carried through the door, warm and concerned. "You up?"

"Coming!" I called, hastily shoving my scrying materials into a drawer. A measuring cup clattered against the wood, making me wince. My heart was racing, partly from the interrupted vision and partly from the knowledge that Jake was about to walk through my door. I smoothed my hair, took a steadying breath, and tried to look like someone who hadn't spent the morning attempting to divine murder clues from breakfast ingredients.

When I opened the door, Jake and Lucky stood on my porch, both wearing expressions of concern poorly masked by attempted cheerfulness. Jake looked as tired as I felt, with shadows under his eyes and his usual easy smile slightly strained.

Lucky, on the other hand, appeared as ethereal as ever in a flowing purple caftan, her silver hair arranged in an artful twist and secured with what looked like decorative chopsticks. The morning breeze carried the scent of lavender and sage—protection herbs, I realized, just as Pecan had noted.

"Thought you might be up early," Jake said, holding up a paper bag that smelled promisingly of coffee and pastries. "Brought reinforcements. Though from the smell of vanilla in here, you've already started your day."

Lucky swept past him, her eyes sharp despite her dreamy demeanor. "Oh, honey," she said, "you look like you've been up with the owls. Though sometimes night hours are when the veil is thinnest, aren't they? When the world holds its breath and secrets rise like cream to the surface."

"More like never went to bed," I admitted, stepping aside to let them in. The floorboards creaked beneath our feet, a familiar symphony of old wood and settled foundations. Pecan trotted over to greet them, his tail wagging as Jake scratched behind his ears.

Lucky knows, Pecan informed me, leaning into Jake's scratches with obvious pleasure. *She's thinking about scrying patterns and wondering if you've figured out how to use them yet. Also, she brought something in her bag. Something magical. I can smell it. Smells like... old books and starlight, if starlight had a smell.*

I wasn't surprised. Lucky had been friends with my grandfather for decades. I suspected she knew more about our family's abilities than I did. She had that same knowing twinkle in her eye that Grandpa used to get, like she was in on a particularly good joke that the rest of the world hadn't caught yet. Now I knew why.

Jake set the breakfast offerings on my kitchen counter, his eyes falling on the bowl of waffle batter. "Already back at it, huh?" He looked worried, probably thinking I was pushing myself too hard after yesterday's arrest. His hand lingered near the bowl, and I held my breath, wondering if any trace of magic remained visible in the batter.

"Force of habit," I said quickly, moving to distribute coffee cups. The ceramic clinked softly against the counter as I pulled down three mugs.

Lucky drifted over to the counter, her rings catching the morning light as she traced a finger along the bowl's edge. The gesture wasn't casual, I realized. She was testing for residual magic. "Sometimes the best answers come when we're doing what feels most natural to us," she said mysteriously. Then, brightening, "Speaking of which, I brought my cards. Thought we might all use a little clarity this morning."

She's going to use the cards to confirm what you saw in the vision, Pecan observed, settling under the table. *Clever. Jake won't question it because he thinks it's just Lucky being Lucky.*

Jake chuckled, already unpacking breakfast—an assortment of muffins and danishes from Sweetie's Bakery that made my stomach rumble despite my anxiety. The scent of cinnamon and butter filled the kitchen, mixing with the lingering vanilla from my scrying attempt. "Lucky and her tarot cards. She read mine once and predicted I'd meet a mysterious woman who'd turn my life upside down." He glanced at me, his smile softening. "Though I suppose she wasn't wrong about that part."

Heat crept into my cheeks as I busied myself with the coffeemaker.

Lucky was already settling at my kitchen table, producing her worn tarot deck from one of her voluminous pockets. The cards looked ancient, their edges soft with use, and I could have sworn they gave off a faint golden glow. The backs were decorated with an intricate pattern of stars and moons that seemed to shift if you looked at them too long.

"The cards don't lie," she said, shuffling with practiced ease. "They just sometimes take their sweet time making sense. Rather like people, wouldn't you say?"

She's doing this on purpose, Pecan observed, settling under the table where he could watch everyone's feet. *The cards are just for show. Well, mostly. She wants to tell you something without alerting Jake. Also, she's got rose quartz in her left pocket and something that smells like cedar in her right. Protection stones, if I know my magic.*

We gathered around the table, armed with coffee and pastries. My grandmother's old lace curtains cast delicate shadows across the tablecloth, creating patterns that seemed to dance around Lucky's cards as she laid them out.

The spread she chose was complex, cards arranged in a pattern that reminded me of a spider's web. Each card was placed with deliberate care. The first card she turned over made my breath catch. Death, its skeletal figure somehow more ominous in the cheerful morning light.

"Don't worry, dear," Lucky said, noting my reaction. "Death rarely means physical death in the cards. It's about transformation, endings that lead to beginnings." She turned over the next card. The Moon, with its howling wolves and hidden paths. "Now this... this is interesting."

Jake leaned forward, his coffee forgotten. Despite his skepticism about divination, I could see curiosity in his eyes. "What does it mean?"

"Deception," Lucky murmured, tapping the Moon card with one ring-laden finger. "Someone's wearing a mask, hiding their true nature." Her finger moved to the next card she revealed. The Tower, where illustrated figures fell from a lightning-struck building. "And here, a sudden revelation, a truth that will shake foundations. The cards speak of hidden dangers and buried secrets."

She's seeing the same thing you did in the batter, Pecan observed, his mental voice tinged with excitement. *Something about that vendor booth you saw. The cards are showing the same pattern. And there's something else... Lucky's thoughts keep circling back to some kind of protection spell she cast last night. She's worried about you, Maple.*

Jake leaned forward, studying the cards with a mix of skepticism and curiosity.

"So someone at the festival isn't who they seem to be?" he asked, his voice low and thoughtful.

"More than that," I said, the pieces aligning in my mind like a perfect waffle pattern. The vision from the batter merged with Lucky's cards, creating a clearer picture. "I think Felix might have discovered something about one of the vendors. Something worth killing over. Something bigger than bad reviews and blackmail."

Lucky turned over another card. The Seven of Swords, showing a figure sneaking away with stolen weapons. "Yes," she murmured. "Something stolen, something hidden. The cards suggest deception layered upon deception."

Jake pulled out his phone, scrolling through what looked like notes. I could see the fatigue lines around his eyes, evidence of a sleepless night spent poring over Felix's notebook. "I've been thinking about that. The festival's competitive, sure, but murder seems extreme. Unless..." He paused, frowning at his screen. "Unless it wasn't just about the festival. What if someone was using the event as cover for something else?"

He's onto something, Pecan commented, his tail thumping against the floor. *His thoughts are jumping between the notebook entries and something he noticed about delivery schedules. Jake might not have magic, but he's got good instincts.*

Lucky gathered her cards with deliberate movements, her bangles chiming softly. "The cards suggest a connection to food or drink, something consumed, but not where you'd expect." She fixed me with a meaningful look. "Sometimes the most important ingredients are the ones we don't see."

"Felix was sampling food all day," I said, remembering the vision in the batter. The image of him standing at that mysterious booth flashed through my mind again. "He stopped at multiple booths before mine." I wrapped my hands around my coffee cup, letting its warmth ground me. "And according to his notebook, he had his fingers in multiple pies, so to speak."

Jake's expression turned thoughtful. "We should retrace his steps. Figure out everywhere he went that morning before..." He trailed off, but we all knew how that sentence ended.

"The festival layout might help," I suggested, reaching for my phone to pull up the vendor map. "If we could—"

The sudden trill of my phone made us all jump. Even Pecan's head snapped up, his ears perking forward. Detective Radcliffe's name flashed on the screen, and my stomach did an uncomfortable flip as I answered.

"Ms. Winslow," Radcliffe's voice was professionally neutral, with just a hint of that smug satisfaction that made me want to dump waffle batter over his head. "I'm calling to inform you that your Waffle Wagon has been cleared to reopen, pending the ongoing investigation."

"That's... thank you," I managed, surprised. I hadn't expected this concession, especially not so soon after my arrest. Jake and Lucky watched me intently, while Pecan pressed closer to my legs.

"Don't thank me yet," Radcliffe replied, and I could practically hear his self-satisfied smile. "And don't leave town. We're still processing evidence, and I'll have more questions for you soon. Consider this a... courtesy."

He's lying, Pecan's thoughts cut through my confusion. *He's hoping you'll lead him to something. Or someone. I can hear it in his thoughts. He's watching you, Maple.*

The line went dead before I could respond. I looked up to find Jake and Lucky watching me expectantly.

"They're letting me reopen the Waffle Wagon," I said, still processing the news. The words felt strange in my mouth, like batter that hadn't quite set.

Jake's face lit up, some of his exhaustion falling away. "That's great!" Then, noting my expression, "Isn't it?"

But Lucky's expression remained serious, her fingers still resting on her tarot deck. "They're hoping you'll lead them to something, or someone," she said softly, echoing Pecan's warning. "Be careful, dear. Sometimes when we're searching for answers, we attract the attention of those who'd rather keep their secrets hidden." She pulled one final card from her deck. The High Priestess, keeper of mysteries. "Trust your intuition, Maple. It runs deeper than you know."

She's right, Pecan added, his mental voice tinged with concern. *But we're getting closer to the truth. I can feel it. That vision you saw in the batter, it means something. We just need to figure out which vendor Felix visited before he came to you.*

"Well," I said, standing up and gathering our empty coffee cups, the ceramic clinking softly against each other, "if they want me to keep working, I'd better get ready to open. Those waffles won't make themselves." The familiar phrase felt like armor, a reminder of who I was and what I stood for.

Jake rose too. "I'll help you set up."

Lucky began packing away her cards. "I'll be around too, dear." She patted her bag meaningfully. "And I might have a few tricks of my own to share."

CHAPTER 12

I methodically prepared the Waffle Wagon for another day of business. My hands moved through the motions, measuring flour, cracking eggs, testing waffle irons, while my mind kept circling back to Detective Radcliffe's suspicious phone call.

The festival grounds were still mostly empty, caught in that space between night and day when everything feels slightly unreal. A few early birds moved between the vendor stalls, setting up their displays or accepting deliveries.

He's been watching the truck for twenty minutes now, Pecan observed from his cushion near the prep area. *Third row of the parking lot, that blue sedan. He's trying to be subtle, but his coffee cup keeps catching the sunlight. Also, he's on his second breakfast sandwich, and it's not even eight o'clock.*

I resisted the urge to look, focusing instead on measuring ingredients into my batter bowl. "Wonderful. Nothing says 'innocent until proven guilty' like police surveillance with a side of breakfast."

At least he picked a decent stake-out spot. Good sight lines, morning shade. Though his choice in music is questionable. Who listens to polka at seven in the morning? Wait. Now it's yacht rock. I'm not sure which is worse.

I was grateful for Pecan's attempt at levity. The morning light streamed through the truck's windows, creating patterns on the stainless steel counters. Everything looked deceptively normal, as if yesterday's arrest had been just a bad dream.

"Maybe we should put on a show," I mused, whisking the batter with perhaps more vigor than necessary. "Dance around the truck, act suspicious. Really give him something to write in his report."

Oh yes, because suspicious behavior is exactly what we need right now. Though I wouldn't mind seeing you attempt the polka. Your dancing skills are almost as questionable as your taste in—

A throat cleared behind me, making me jump. Vanilla extract sloshed over my fingers as I spun around, coming face to face with the last person I expected to see. Sassy, owner of the Crepe Queen food truck and a longtime festival rival.

The sight of her in my truck was so unexpected that for a moment, I just stared. She looked... different. Her usual perfectly coiffed appearance seemed slightly disheveled, her trademark red lipstick missing. The designer outfit was still there. Some sort of silk blouse and tailored pants that probably cost more than my monthly rent. But she wore it like armor that was cracking.

Her fingers twisted the strap of her handbag, a nervous gesture that seemed completely at odds with her usual confident demeanor.

"We need to talk," she said, glancing over her shoulder. "Privately."

She's worried about something, Pecan noted. *Her thoughts are all jumbled, but I keep catching Felix's name. And something about bank statements? She's trying very hard not to think about specific details.*

I studied Sassy's face, searching for any sign of deception. Our relationship had always been more sour than sweet. She'd spent years trying to edge my grandfather's business out of the festival circuit, using everything from health code complaints to negative social media campaigns. Now here she was, standing in my food truck, looking like she'd rather be anywhere else.

"Why should I trust you?" I asked, wiping my hands with a dish towel. The scent of sweetness lingered in the air between us, mixing with what I recognized as her signature expensive perfume. "Last I checked, you were telling anyone who'd listen that my waffles were 'pedestrian at best' and suggesting the health department should do a surprise inspection."

A flash of her usual fire sparked in her eyes, and for a moment, I saw the familiar Sassy. The one who'd once tried to convince the festival board that waffle trucks should be relegated to the "budget food" section. "They are pedestrian. And your setup could use a thorough inspection. But that's not—" She caught herself, took a deep breath that seemed to cost her something. "Look, I'm not here because I suddenly want to be besties and braid each other's hair. I'm here be cause..." She glanced around again, lowering her voice to barely above a whisper. "Because Felix had dirt on me, too."

She's telling the truth, Pecan confirmed, sitting up straighter on his cushion. *And there's more she's not saying yet. Something about financial troubles and family reputation. Also, she's terrified someone might see her here. Her thoughts keep jumping to what her mother would say if this got out.*

I moved to close the service window, drawing the curtain for privacy. The familiar sounds of the festival setting up became muffled, creating a strange bubble of intimacy in the truck. "Go on."

Sassy sank onto my prep stool, her designer bag sliding to the floor with a soft thud. She didn't even seem to notice when it landed in a small puddle of spilled vanilla extract. "Two years ago, my business almost went under. The festival circuit was down, and I had just invested in a second truck. I made some... questionable decisions with the books. Nothing illegal," she added quickly, her fingers twisting together in her lap. "Just creative accounting to keep things afloat. Felix somehow found out."

"He blackmailed you," I said, the pieces clicking into place like a perfect waffle pattern.

She nodded, her perfectly manicured nails drumming against my counter in an erratic rhythm. "Monthly payments to keep quiet. Plus inside information about other vendors, tips about health code violations, that sort of thing. He said if I didn't play along, he'd make sure every food magazine and blog knew about my financial troubles. Do you have any idea what that would do to my family's reputation? The Bright name has been in the restaurant business for three generations."

I leaned against the opposite counter, processing this new information. "How much did he take?"

"Too much." Her laugh was bitter, empty of humor. "But it wasn't just about the money. He wanted control. Information. Power." She looked up at me, and for the first time, I saw past her carefully maintained facade to something raw and genuine. "When I heard he was dead, I was relieved. Then I was terrified, because what if someone found his records? What if everything came out, anyway?"

There's something else, Pecan interjected, his ears perking forward. *She knows about other vendors Felix targeted. She's debating whether to tell you. And there's something about a notebook – not the one Jake has, a different one.*

I grabbed my coffee pot, pouring two cups. The rich aroma filled the small space, offering a moment of normalcy in this surreal conversation. Sassy accepted hers with a surprised look, as if she'd expected me to throw her out. Her fingers curled around the mug. I noticed they were trembling slightly.

"You're not the only one he was blackmailing, are you?" I kept my voice gentle, like I was coaxing a scared animal.

She wrapped her hands tighter around the mug, the steam rising between us like a veil. "No. I know of at least three others. Maybe more. He had this... system. He'd watch people, learn their weaknesses, their secrets. Then he'd strike when they were most vulnerable."

"Names?"

She shook her head, some of her usual steel returning to her spine. "Not yet. I need to be sure I can trust you first." Her eyes met mine, steady and serious. "And you need to be sure you can trust me. We both know our history isn't exactly friendly."

She has a point, Pecan observed, moving closer to sniff at Sassy's designer shoes. *Though I can tell she's genuinely scared. Whatever she knows, it's big enough to make her come to you for help. Also, her shoes are real leather. Very expensive. She must have been paying Felix a fortune to keep quiet.*

I took a sip of coffee, buying time to think. Through the curtained window, I could hear the festival coming to life. Somewhere out there, Detective Radcliffe was watching, waiting for me to make a mistake.

"Why come to me now?" I asked finally, setting my mug down with a soft clink. "Why not when Felix was alive?"

Sassy's fingers tightened around her mug until her knuckles went white. "Because whoever killed him knew about his blackmail scheme. They had to. And that means they might know about all of us, everyone he was controlling." She set the mug down with a sharp click that made us both wince. "Look, I don't like you. You don't like me. But right now, we both need answers. And..." she hesitated, seeming to struggle with what she was about to say. "And you're the only one actually trying to find the truth instead of just accepting what the police want to believe."

I thought about Jake's theory that the festival was being used as cover for something bigger. About Lucky's cards warning of deception layered upon deception. About that mysterious booth I'd seen in my scrying vision. The pieces were there, but the picture they formed was still frustratingly unclear.

"If we do this," I said slowly, measuring each word like ingredients in a recipe, "we do it my way. No games, no holding back information. Complete honesty, even if it's uncomfortable. Deal?"

She considered this, her business sense visibly warring with her desperation. Finally, she nodded. "Deal. But this stays between us. I can't risk—"

A sharp knock on the truck's side door made us both jump. Coffee sloshed over the rims of our mugs as Sassy's bag toppled completely into the vanilla puddle.

"Ms. Winslow?" Detective Radcliffe's voice carried through the metal with suspicious clarity. "Mind if we have a word?"

He's suspicious about why your truck isn't open yet, Pecan reported, his tail tucking slightly. *And he recognized Sassy going in. He's thinking about how convenient it is that two of his suspects are meeting in private. Quick, she needs to hide!*

I gestured frantically at the small storage area behind the prep station, mouthing "Hide!" Sassy moved with surprising agility for someone in designer heels, tucking herself out of sight just as I opened the door.

"Detective," I said, trying to sound surprised rather than panicked. "What brings you by so early? I was just about to open up."

He fake smiled, his eyes busy scanning every inch of my truck's interior. "Just checking in. Making sure everything's... up to code." His gaze lingered on the two coffee cups on the counter. "Thought I saw Sassy Bright come this way. You two aren't exactly known for being friendly."

"Oh?" I widened my eyes innocently, channeling my best confused look. "I haven't seen her. Though she usually sets up around this time. Her truck's just down the row." I gestured vaguely in that direction, hoping he wouldn't notice the designer bag partially hidden behind my prep station.

He's not buying it, Pecan warned. *But he can't prove anything either. He's wondering if you two are conspiring about Felix. Also, he really needs to switch cologne brands. That stuff smells like my flea medication.*

"Right." Radcliffe's smile tightened into something that looked almost painful. "Well, don't let me keep you from your setup. Though I have to say, it's interesting how quickly you're back to business after everything that's happened. Most people might take a day or two to... reflect."

"Innocent people don't hide, Detective," I replied, matching his smile with one of my own. "And waffles wait for no one. Was there anything else you needed?"

He lingered a moment longer, his presence filling the doorway like a storm cloud. "Just remember what I said about staying in town, Ms. Winslow. We wouldn't want any... complications."

I waited until he was well away from the truck before closing the door. Sassy emerged from hiding, brushing dust from her silk blouse with a look of absolute disgust.

"Well," she said dryly, retrieving her now vanilla-scented designer bag, "that was cozy. Does he always lurk around like that?"

"Only since he decided I'm a murderer." I moved to the window, peeking through the curtain to make sure Radcliffe was really gone. His blue sedan was still visible in the parking lot, but at least he wasn't actively watching the truck anymore. "So, about those other vendors Felix was blackmailing..."

Sassy straightened her clothes, recovering some of her usual poise. "I'll need to be careful how I approach them. Some might talk to me, but others..." She shook her head, tucking a stray strand of hair behind her ear. "Give me some time. I'll see what I can find out."

"And I'm just supposed to trust that you'll come back?" I started wiping down the counter, trying to clean up the evidence of our impromptu meeting.

"Please." She rolled her eyes with a familiar hint of her usual disdain. "If I was going to run, I wouldn't have come to you in the first place.

Besides," she added, her voice dropping, "we both know Detective Radcliffe is probably going to have someone following both of us now."

She's right about that, Pecan commented, moving to his observation post by the window. *There's already another unmarked car pulling into the lot. These police officers really need to work on their subtlety.*

Sassy picked up her bag, then paused, her hand on the door handle. "There is one thing. The morning Felix died, before he came to your truck, I saw him talking to someone by the east entrance. They seemed... intense. Not his usual smug interrogation style."

My heart quickened. The east entrance. That matched my scrying vision perfectly. "Who was it?"

"I couldn't tell. They were partly hidden behind one of the vendor tents. But..." She frowned, concentration creasing her forehead. "There was something familiar about them. The way they moved, maybe? And Felix looked scared. Really scared. Not his usual performative outrage, but genuine fear."

She's remembering something else, Pecan said suddenly, his tail twitching with interest. *Something about papers changing hands.*

"Was there anything else unusual that morning?" I pressed, trying to keep my voice casual. "Anything out of place? Even small details might help."

Her forehead creased deeper as she thought. "Now that you mention it... there was a delivery van parked where it shouldn't have been. By the service entrance. White, unmarked. I remember thinking it was odd because all the morning deliveries were already done." She paused, then added, "And it was blocking my usual parking spot, which is why I noticed it at all."

"Did you see who was driving it?"

"No, but..." She hesitated, then reached into her bag and pulled out her phone. After a few swipes, she turned it toward me. "I took a picture because I was going to complain to festival management about unauthorized vehicles. Never got around to it, but..."

The photo showed a white van, partially obscured by morning fog. No markings, no company name, just a dent in the rear bumper shaped like a crescent moon.

"Send that to me," I said, trying to keep the excitement out of my voice. Finally, actual evidence of something concrete.

The van matches the one I saw in the parking lot yesterday, Pecan added. *The one that left right after Felix's body was found.*

I filed this information away, adding it to my mental map of that morning's events. "If you think of anything else..."

"I'll let you know." She moved toward the door, then turned back. "For what it's worth, I don't think you killed him. You're not that clever." A ghost of her old smirk appeared. "Besides, if you were going to murder someone, you'd probably do it with those awful cheese waffles of yours. Much more obvious."

I like her, Pecan declared as Sassy slipped out of the truck. *She's mean, but she's honest about being mean. And she really does want to help, even if she'd rather eat raw flour than admit it. Plus, she scratched behind my ears when she thought you weren't looking.*

I watched through the window as Sassy made her way back to her own truck. No one watching would guess she'd just formed an alliance with her biggest rival.

"Well," I muttered, turning back to my neglected waffle batter, "I guess we're adding 'unlikely partnerships' to our list of daily specials."

Speaking of specials, Pecan stretched lazily on his cushion, *you might want to actually open soon. There's a line forming, and Detective Radcliffe is still watching. Though his polka music has switched to country western, which might actually be worse. Also, that couple at the front of the line has been arguing about whether to get chocolate chip or blueberry waffles for ten minutes straight.*

I took a deep breath, centering myself in the familiar routine of my kitchen. Sassy's information had given us new leads, but it had also confirmed something unsettling. Felix's web of blackmail and secrets ran deeper than anyone suspected. Jake wouldn't believe that now I had an unexpected ally in the search.

Just remember, Pecan added as I poured the first waffle of the day, watching the batter spread into its familiar pattern, *if Sassy tries to double-cross us, I reserve the right to shed all over her designer shoes. And maybe leave a few surprise presents near her truck. You know, just to maintain our professional rivalry.*

CHAPTER 13

After the morning's drama with Sassy and Detective Radcliffe's surveillance, the festival's post-lunch lull felt almost surreal. The crowds had thinned to a gentle trickle, giving me a moment to breathe and process everything that had happened.

That's the third time you've reorganized those napkins, Pecan observed from his cushion. *I'm pretty sure they're as alphabetized as they're going to get.*

"I'm not alphabetizing them," I protested, realizing I had indeed been sorting them by color intensity. "I'm just... thinking."

About Sassy's revelation? Or the mysterious van? Or maybe about how Detective Radcliffe has switched to listening to show tunes? Because that last one is particularly disturbing.

I was about to respond when the familiar tap of sensible shoes caught my attention. There, climbing the steps to my truck with surprising agility for her age, was Ellie Thistlewood. She carried a wicker basket that filled the air with the kind of warmth that usually only came from childhood memories.

She bakes when she's worried, Pecan observed, lifting his head with interest. *And judging by the size of that basket, she's very worried indeed. Also, she's wearing her good brooch. The one she only wears to committee meetings and special occasions.*

"Maple, dear," Ellie's voice carried the warmth of a grandmother's hugs. "I thought you might need a pick-me-up." She set the basket on my counter, the red and white checkered cloth covering it as pristine as her pressed floral dress.

"Ellie," I smiled, genuinely pleased to see her familiar face. "You didn't have to bring me anything."

"Nonsense." She waved away my protest with one well-manicured hand. "Everyone needs cookies during difficult times. And heaven knows, you've had your share of difficulties lately." Her eyes, sharp despite their kindly crinkles, took in every detail of my truck's interior.

She's cataloging everything, Pecan noted. *The way she looks around, it's like she's solving a puzzle in her head. And she's noticed at least three things we thought we'd hidden. Never underestimate the observational skills of someone who's been judging church bake sales for forty years.*

I pulled out my spare stool, the one Jake usually claimed during his visits. The metal legs squeaked slightly against the floor, a sound that seemed too harsh in the gentle afternoon quiet. "Would you like some tea? I just put on a fresh pot."

"That would be lovely, dear." Ellie settled onto the stool with the grace of someone who'd spent years making herself comfortable in other people's spaces. She began unpacking her basket, revealing rows of perfectly uniform cookies that made my professional baker's heart a little jealous. Each one was exactly the same size, with an ideal ratio of cinnamon to sugar coating. "I made snickerdoodles. Your grandfather always said they were his favorite."

The mention of Henry caught me off guard. "You knew my grandfather well?"

"Oh yes," she smiled, accepting the tea I offered."Henry and I go way back. We served on the festival committee together for years. Such a kind man, and clever too. He could always tell when something wasn't quite right at the festival."

Her words carried weight beyond their surface meaning. I took a cookie. The taste brought back memories of childhood visits to the festival, when everything seemed simpler and the biggest drama was whether we'd run out of whipped cream before closing time.

She's thinking about Felix, Pecan suddenly interjected. *And something about committee meetings from last year. She's seen more than she lets on.*

"The festival's changed a lot since then," I ventured carefully, watching Ellie's face. The afternoon light softened her wrinkles but couldn't hide the knowing look in her eyes.

"Mmm." She took a delicate sip of tea. "Change isn't always for the better, is it? Take poor Felix, for instance. When he first started reviewing for the festival, he had such passion for food. Such genuine enthusiasm." Her eyes grew distant, focused on something beyond the festival crowds outside my window. "But power has a way of corrupting even the most genuine passions."

I nearly dropped my cookie. "You knew about Felix's... activities?"

Ellie's laugh was soft, but knowing. "I didn't know him personally, but I've heard things." She arranged her cookies with precise movements, each one aligned perfectly with its neighbors.

She's got dirt on everyone, Pecan marveled. *All those years of serving coffee at committee meetings, and people just... talked around her. Like she was part of the furniture. The things she must know about this town could fill a recipe book – and not the kind you'd want to share at a church social.*

"Did you ever..." I hesitated, not wanting to offend her.

"Report him?" Ellie finished my thought, her voice gentle but firm. "I didn't really have any concrete evidence." She sighed, and for a moment, I saw the weight of years of silent observation in her expression. "Besides, there were... complications. The kind that make you question whether the right thing and the kind thing are always the same."

"Complications?"

She nodded, reaching for her tea again. "Felix had a nephew—has a nephew. Timothy. Sweet boy, only twelve. He's been fighting a rare form of leukemia for the past three years. The treatments are experimental, expensive. Insurance won't cover most of it." She paused, stirring her tea though she hadn't added any sugar. "I heard Felix was trying to help him."

The revelation hit me like a badly timed waffle flip, leaving my thoughts scattered and messy. "Felix was using the blackmail money for his nephew's treatment?"

"Some of it, at least." Ellie's voice held a mix of sympathy and disapproval. "It doesn't excuse what he did, of course. But sometimes desperate people make desperate choices. They start with just a little compromise, like adding just a touch more sugar to balance a bitter taste. But before they know it, the whole recipe is altered beyond recognition."

She paused, selecting another cookie with careful deliberation. "Though I suspect Timothy's treatments weren't the only reason for his... fundraising efforts. There were other hands in that cookie jar, so to speak."

She's holding something back, Pecan warned. *A name she's trying very hard not to think about.*

I leaned forward slightly, the counter cool under my palms. "What do you mean?"

Ellie's eyes met mine, sharp and clear as cut crystal. "Let's just say that Felix's influence extended beyond the festival circuit. He had connections, powerful ones. People who used his position to gather information, to apply pressure where needed." She brushed cookie crumbs from her lap with precise movements. "The festival was just one piece of a larger puzzle."

The words echoed Jake's theory about the festival being used as a cover for something bigger. "Did you ever see him meeting with these connections?"

"Now and then." She smiled. "I had my suspicions, but I just couldn't get involved."

My heart skipped.

"I see a lot of things, dear." Ellie's voice remained gentle, but there was steel beneath the softness. "The advantage of being my age is that people tend to look right through you." She set her teacup down with a decisive clink.

"Do you think there's something that would help? If you know anything that could point Detective Radcliffe to the real killer."

She's worried about telling you anything, Pecan observed. *Her thoughts keep jumping to other festival volunteers, people she's known for years. She's not sure who to trust anymore. There's something about missing committee records too.*

"Ellie," I said softly, "why are you telling me all this now?"

She reached across the counter to pat my hand, her skin soft and paper-thin over bird-like bones. "Because your grandfather would have wanted someone looking out for you. And because sometimes the most dangerous secrets are the ones we think we've buried deepest." Her grip tightened slightly. "Be careful, dear. Not everyone at this festival is who they appear to be."

"Are you worried about someone specific?"

Her smile turned sad, like frosting on a farewell cake. "I'm worried about a lot of things, dear. About what Felix's death might uncover. About what it might bury deeper." She stood, smoothing her dress with practiced grace. "Keep the cookies. Share them with that handsome mechanic friend of yours. Jake, isn't it?"

She's deflecting, Pecan noted. *But there's genuine concern there too. She cares about what happens to you.*

"Thank you," I said, walking her to the door. "For the cookies, and for..."

"For being a nosy old woman who can't mind her own business?" Her eyes twinkled like sugar crystals. "You're welcome." She paused at the top step, adjusting her brooch with deliberate care.

She descended the steps and merged into the festival crowd, her floral dress and sensible shoes making her just another face in the afternoon bustle.

Well, Pecan stretched lazily, *that was illuminating. And slightly terrifying. Who knew the cookie lady was basically running her own intelligence operation?*

I picked up Ellie's teacup, still warm from her hands. "What did you get from her thoughts? Anything specific about who Felix was meeting with?"

She was being very careful with her thoughts, Pecan admitted. *Though she slipped once . And she kept thinking about the festival's financial reports, but I couldn't catch why.*

"We need to check out that empty booth I saw in my scrying," I decided, already mentally calculating when I could slip away from the truck. "And we need to look into the festival's financial records."

Great, Pecan sighed. *More sneaking around. More mysterious documents. More chances for Detective Radcliffe to add to his 'Maple is Suspicious' file. Though I suppose it beats sitting here watching him listen to his terrible music choices. He's moved on to 80s power ballads now, by the way. The man's musical taste is as questionable as his investigative skills.*

Ellie's warning echoed in my mind.

You know, Pecan mused, *for someone who bakes such comforting cookies, Ellie gives remarkably unsettling warnings. Though I suppose that's rather fitting for this festival lately. Everything sweet seems to come with a side of danger. Also,* he added, his tail wagging hopefully, *I think we should definitely sample more of these cookies. For investigative purposes, of course.*

CHAPTER 14

I busied myself with preparations for the next wave of festival customers.

Speaking of secrets, Pecan's voice drifted into my thoughts, *your favorite elderly informant seems to have found another confidant. And judging by his thoughts, he's definitely fishing for more than just festival gossip.*

Following his gaze through the truck's serving window, I spotted Ellie pausing near the festival's information booth, deep in conversation with a familiar face I couldn't quite place.

That's Jesse Hart, Pecan supplied helpfully, his mental voice tinged with amusement. *The reporter who covered the book launch.*

The memory clicked into place. As I watched, he nodded earnestly at whatever Ellie was saying, his notebook conspicuously absent but his attention completely focused. The way he kept his hands loose at his sides reminded me of a poker player trying not to reveal his tells.

"I didn't know Ellie knew him," I murmured, absently reorganizing my syrup bottles. The glass clinked softly as I lined them up by flavor.

Oh, they're related, Pecan stretched lazily on his cushion, his tail thumping against the side of the truck. *He's thinking about Sunday dinners at 'Aunt Ellie's' and something about her famous pot roast. Though right now he's more interested in why she just spent twenty minutes in your truck. Also, he's had three cups of coffee already today, and he's planning on a fourth. The man's basically a caffeine sponge.*

A group of festival-goers passed by, their chatter momentarily drowning out the ambient sounds. I used their presence as cover to observe Jesse more carefully.

Before I could process this new information, Jesse was making his way toward the Waffle Wagon. He moved with the practiced ease of someone used to making himself appear harmless while missing nothing.

"Maple Winslow," he called out, flashing a smile that probably worked wonders on his sources. The late afternoon sun caught the press badge hanging from his neck, making it glint like a warning signal. "I was hoping I might catch you between the lunch and dinner rush."

I kept my own smile professional, neither too warm nor too distant, while quickly wiping down my already clean counter. "Hello, Jesse. Looking for a waffle fix?"

He climbed the steps to my truck with the confidence of someone used to inserting himself into other people's spaces. The metal stairs creaked slightly under his weight, a sound that seemed to emphasize the intrusion. "And while I wouldn't say no to one of your famous creations, that apple-cinnamon special I keep hearing about, maybe? I actually wanted to properly introduce myself. I see you've already met my Aunt Ellie."

"Aunt Ellie?" I echoed, though Pecan had already confirmed this connection. Sometimes playing slightly naive was the best way to handle reporters.

He's trying to read your reaction, Pecan observed, lifting his head from his cushion. *Watching to see if you'll let slip anything Ellie might have told you. Journalists and their psychological games – it's like watching a cat pretend it's not hunting the canary.*

Jesse leaned against my counter, his posture deliberately casual but his eyes missing nothing. "She speaks very highly of you and your grandfather. Henry was something of a legend in this town. Did you know he once convinced the entire festival committee to hold a midnight waffle-making contest during a power outage? Used camping stoves and everything."

"He was full of surprises," I agreed, pouring batter onto the iron with practiced precision. "Though I'm sure you know that, having covered local events."

"True," he chuckled, his laugh practiced. "Though I prefer getting firsthand accounts whenever possible. Speaking of which..." He paused, his expression shifting to something more serious. "This business with Felix Montclair – it must be quite challenging for a new business owner."

Smooth transition, Pecan snorted. *About as subtle as a food fight at a wedding. Also, he's got at least three different angles planned for this story, depending on what you give him. Journalists really are fascinating creatures – like squirrels hoarding nuts, except it's secrets.*

I measured my response carefully while flipping the waffle. Steam rose between us like a barrier. "It's been difficult for everyone involved with the festival. Felix had... quite an impact on the community."

"That's one way to put it," Jesse's eyes sparkled with interest as he watched me plate his waffle. "Though I imagine some impacts were more positive than others. There are quite a few vendors who seem remarkably... unburdened by his passing. Nina from the cheese shop, for instance, seems to have developed quite a spring in her step."

The conversation was starting to feel like a dance where I couldn't quite hear the music. "I try not to speculate about other people's reactions to tragedy. Grief affects everyone differently." I handed him his waffle, perfectly golden and dressed with a light dusting of powdered sugar.

He's fishing, Pecan warned, his mental voice tense. *And thinking about something Ellie told him about Felix's last morning. Something about an envelope... but he's being careful not to focus on it too directly. It's like he's got mental sticky notes scattered all over the place.*

Before I could probe that particular thread, movement caught my eye. Sassy emerged from her food truck. Her path seemed to be leading directly toward Jesse. And the way she moved, confident, purposeful, with just a hint of extra sway, suggested this wasn't their first interaction.

"Jesse Hart," Sassy called out, her voice carrying that special tone reserved for people she found useful. The same tone she'd used with me when suggesting our alliance. "Don't tell me you're trying to scoop my exclusive?"

Jesse turned, his smile shifting from professional to personal so smoothly it was almost imperceptible. Almost. "Wouldn't dream of it, Sass. Just making family connections." He took a bite of his waffle, his eyebrows rising in appreciation. "Though I might have to write about these waffles. They're even better than the rumors suggest."

The casual nickname hung in the air. I watched them carefully while pretending to adjust my temperature settings.

Well, well, Pecan mused, sitting up straighter. *Looks like someone's been doing more than just investigating local cuisine. Their thoughts are practically tap-dancing around each other. She's thinking about some late-night interview at The Copper Kettle last week, and he's remembering something about sharing crepes after hours. Very cozy for a professional relationship.*

Sassy reached us, positioning herself carefully between Jesse and my truck. "Maple, honey, I hope Jesse here isn't bothering you with his reporter routine. He can be rather persistent when he smells a story." She laughed, but there was an edge to it, like a knife wrapped in silk.

"Just getting to know my aunt's friends," Jesse protested, though his eyes never lost their calculating edge. He dabbed at his mouth with a napkin, the gesture somehow making him look more like a predator pausing between bites than a man finishing his breakfast. "Speaking of which, Sass, we should finish our discussion about that feature piece. The one about local food truck entrepreneurs facing adversity?"

The way he emphasized 'adversity' made my stomach twist. I wondered how much of that story she'd already shared with Jesse.

"Of course," Sassy smiled, but I caught the quick glance she threw my way. Something passed between them, silent but significant.

She's trying to damage control, Pecan observed. *Her thoughts are bouncing between worry about what you might have told Jesse and hope that she can spin this story her way.*

As they moved away, their heads bent close in conversation, I felt the first real stirrings of doubt about my alliance with Sassy. The easy familiarity between her and Jesse spoke of shared confidences. And in my experience, reporters rarely kept secrets without using them. Their figures merged into the festival crowd.

The sound of heavy boots on my truck's steps interrupted my brooding. Jake appeared. "You look like someone just told you they prefer pancakes," he said, claiming his usual spot on the spare stool. "Everything okay?"

I glanced around, making sure we were relatively alone. The carousel music in the distance provided perfect cover for quiet conversation.

He's worried about you, Pecan noted. *He noticed Jesse talking to you earlier. Also, he fixed Mrs. Peterson's car in record time just to get here sooner. Not that he's thinking about telling you that part.*

"Remember that notebook Pecan found in Felix's things?" I kept my voice low, busying myself with preparing Jake's usual coffee order.

His expression turned serious, the playful glint in his eyes replaced by concern. He leaned forward, dropping his voice to match my quiet tone. "The one with all the names and numbers? Yeah, it's still in my toolbox at the shop. Been trying to figure out what to do with it. Those numbers..." He shook his head. "Some of them are pretty significant."

"I think..." I paused, watching steam rise from the coffee cup between us. "I think we need to turn it over to Detective Radcliffe."

Are we sure about this? Pecan's mental voice carried a note of concern. *Once we hand it over, we lose control of that information. And Radcliffe isn't exactly your biggest fan right now.*

Jake nodded slowly. "Actually, I've been thinking the same thing. But you know Radcliffe's going to want to know where it came from. He's been watching this place like a hawk with a badge and a bad attitude."

"That's why I think you should be the one to turn it in," I said, the plan forming as I spoke. "You could say you found it while working on festival maintenance, maybe near where Felix was last seen."

He considered this, taking a thoughtful sip of coffee. "It could work. Make it look like Felix dropped it that morning. And coming from me..."

"I hope it won't add to Radcliffe's suspicions about me," I finished. A group of teenagers passed by, laughing about something on their phones, and we both waited until they were out of earshot before continuing.

He's running through scenarios in his head, Pecan observed. *Calculating the best way to present it to Radcliffe. He's actually pretty good at this whole subterfuge thing. Must be all that practice helping customers understand their car repairs without panicking them.*

Jake's eyes met mine, concern evident in their depths. "You sure about this? Once it's in official hands, we can't control what happens next. And some of those names in the notebook..." He trailed off meaningfully.

"I'm sure," I said, though my stomach twisted slightly. "We need to play this smart, and right now, that means appearing cooperative." I adjusted my apron strings, a nervous habit. "Besides, keeping evidence feels a lot like obstruction of justice, and I'd rather not add that to my resume."

Jake finished his coffee and stood, his height casting a shadow across my workspace. "I'll head over to the station now, before I talk myself out of it. The sooner we get this done, the better." He hesitated, then added, "You going to be okay here? Especially with Hart sniffing around?"

I managed a smile, trying to project confidence. "I've got Pecan to keep me company. And apparently, half the town's secrets to sort through." I glanced at the cookie basket Ellie had left. "Plus enough stress-eating material to last through a small crisis."

"Just..." Jake hesitated at the top of the steps, his expression serious. "Be careful, okay? Especially around Hart. That guy's got a way of turning casual conversations into front-page news. I've seen him take down bigger targets than a food truck vendor with just a notebook and a hunch."

He's not wrong, Pecan added. *Jesse's thoughts earlier were like a spider web ,everything connected to everything else, and all of it sticky with potential headlines.*

The festival lights began flickering on early, fighting against the gathering clouds that threatened rain. The evening crowd was filtering in, drawn by the lights and the promise of dinner.

I turned back to my waffle iron, ready to face the dinner rush. After all, as Henry always said, even the most complicated problems could be solved with enough patience, persistence, and properly prepared batter. Though I was pretty sure he'd never had to deal with quite this many layers of mystery in his waffle-making days.

Oh, I wouldn't be so sure about that, Pecan mused, watching a group of customers approach. *The more we learn about this town, the more I think your grandfather knew exactly what he was doing when he left you this truck. Though next time, maybe he could leave us a guidebook for navigating small-town conspiracies. Or at least a recipe for stress-relieving waffles.*

The first drops of rain began to fall, sending festival-goers scurrying for cover. But in my little waffle truck, with Pecan by my side and the notebook finally on its way to proper authorities, I felt oddly calm.

Chapter 15

The quiet felt almost sacred, broken only by the occasional coo of morning doves and the distant hum of early delivery trucks.

Through my truck's serving window, I could see the carousel's horses frozen mid-gallop, their painted eyes somehow more haunting in the early light. The previous day's paper cups and napkins skittered across the ground in the morning breeze, like tumbleweeds in a ghost town.

I was in my usual pre-opening routine, arranging supplies with the methodical precision Grandpa Henry had instilled in me. "A properly organized workspace is half the battle," he used to say, and I could almost hear his voice. My mind wandered to Jake's delivery of Felix's notebook to Detective Radcliffe yesterday, wondering how long it would take before the fallout reached us.

The memory of yesterday's events played through my mind as I worked. The weight of Felix's notebook, filled with its damning evidence. The way Jake had handled the situation with such careful consideration.

The familiar click-clack of Pecan's nails against the pavement broke through my reverie, but something about his approach was different. Instead of his usual morning greeting floating into my thoughts, typically something sarcastic about my early-bird tendencies, he trotted up to the Waffle Wagon with unusual purpose, carrying what looked like an empty syrup bottle in his mouth. His tail wagged with such vigor that his whole body wiggled, clearly proud of his discovery. How had he escaped without my noticing?

"What have you got there, buddy?" I asked, descending the steps to meet him. The metal stairs creaked under my feet, the sound echoing in the empty festival grounds. He dropped the bottle at my feet with a gentle clunk, looking up at me with expectant eyes. The bottle was sticky, its label partially torn, and something about it made the hair on the back of my neck stand up.

I reached down to pat Pecan's head, my fingers automatically seeking the reassuring touch of his collar. And found nothing but fur. The absence hit me like a physical blow, sending my heart into an immediate panicked rhythm.

"Pecan, where's your collar?" My voice came out higher than intended, panic already bubbling up in my chest. He cocked his head to the side, pawing at the syrup bottle insistently. The silence in my head where his thoughts should have been felt wrong. I'd grown so accustomed to his running commentary, his observations about passing customers, his warnings about approaching trouble, the silence felt deafening.

"No, no, no," I muttered, dropping to my knees to check his neck more thoroughly. The morning dew soaked through my jeans, but I barely noticed. "When did you last have it? Where have you been?" My fingers combed through his fur, searching for any sign of the magical collar that had become such an essential part of our lives. The familiar weight of his thoughts in my mind had become as natural as breathing, and now that connection was just... gone.

I thought back to last night's closing routine. Pecan had been commenting on Mrs. Henderson's new perfume (*Smells like she bathed in a flower shop that exploded*), and making predictions about tomorrow's weather (*My left ear says rain, but my right ear's betting on sunshine*). How had I not noticed when the thoughts stopped?

Pecan whined, nudging the bottle again with his nose. His eyes held that particular intelligence I'd grown so accustomed to, but without the collar, I couldn't access the thoughts behind them. It was like watching a foreign film without subtitles.

"Maple?" Jake's voice carried across the morning air, startling me from my increasingly panicked examination. "You're up early. Everything okay?"

I looked up to find him approaching, two coffee cups in hand, his familiar figure backlit by the rising sun. He must have noticed something in my expression because his smile quickly shifted to concern.

"Pecan's collar is missing," I said, trying to keep my voice steady even as my hands shook slightly. "He brought this bottle, but I can't... I mean, he can't..." I stopped, realizing I couldn't exactly explain that without his magical collar, Pecan couldn't tell me why he thought the bottle was important. How do you tell someone you've lost a magical connection they didn't even know existed?

The festival grounds around us were starting to show the first signs of life. Each sound seemed to emphasize the silence where Pecan's thoughts should be.

Jake set the coffees down on my bottom step and crouched beside me, his movements deliberate, like he was approaching a spooked animal. The leather of his work boots creaked slightly as he settled next to us. "Hey, it's probably just slipped off somewhere nearby. We'll find it."

"You don't understand," I said, then caught myself. Of course he didn't understand. How could he? "That collar was special. It was... it helped us communicate." The words felt inadequate to describe what we'd lost. How could I explain that Pecan wasn't just my dog, but my partner in solving crimes, my early warning system, my constant companion in ways that went beyond the normal human-pet relationship?

Jake's eyes flickered between me and Pecan, something thoughtful crossing his features. In the growing light. I could see the moment when several pieces seemed to click into place in his mind. "I've noticed that, actually. The way you two seem to... understand each other. It's always been a bit more than just regular dog-owner stuff, hasn't it?"

I picked up the bottle Pecan had brought, turning it over in my hands to avoid Jake's perceptive gaze. The glass was cool against my fingers, still holding the night's chill. Something felt off about it. When I brought it to my nose, beneath the sweet maple scent lurked something sharper, almost bitter. The kind of smell that made your instincts scream 'danger' before your brain could process why.

"Something's not right," I said, tilting the bottle toward the growing morning light. "See how the label's been layered? Someone tried to disguise it." The adhesive was different too. Slightly yellowed where it showed through the tears.

Pecan barked once, sharp and insistent, pawing at my knee. His usual eloquent explanations replaced by desperate attempts to communicate through traditional dog behaviors felt like watching someone try to explain quantum physics through charades.

"I think..." I lowered my voice, glancing around the empty festival grounds. The early morning shadows suddenly seemed deeper, more threatening. A golf cart hummed past in the distance, carrying supplies to one of the food stalls. "I think this might be the bottle that killed Felix."

Jake's expression darkened, his easy-going mechanic's demeanor replaced by something more serious. "Are you sure?"

"No, but look at this." I pointed to the partially revealed label underneath mine. "Someone reused one of my bottles, but they did a sloppy job covering the original label. And smell this. There's something else mixed in with the syrup residue. Something that shouldn't be there." The bitter undertone reminded me of almonds, but not quite. Something chemical and wrong.

He took the bottle, examining it with the same careful attention he gave to diagnosing engine problems. His fingers traced the edge of the torn label, and I watched his nostrils flare slightly as he caught the bitter undertone. "Where did you find this, boy?" he asked Pecan, who responded by walking a few steps toward the festival's storage area, then looking back at us expectantly.

The storage area lay behind the main festival grounds, a maze of metal containers and wooden crates that housed everything from spare parts to emergency supplies. During festival hours, it was mostly ignored – a backstage area that guests never saw. But now, in the early morning light, it looked like the perfect place to hide secrets.

"We need to find that collar," I said, standing up and brushing the damp grass from my knees. "It's not just about Pecan. It's about solving this case. Without it..." I trailed off. How do you tell someone you've lost your magical mind-reading dog without sounding completely unhinged?

Somewhere in the distance, a radio started playing, the tinny sound of local morning news mixing with the natural sounds of the festival coming to life.

Jake handed the bottle back to me. "Then we'll find it. The festival doesn't open for another two hours, plenty of time to search."

We followed Pecan as he led us toward the storage area, weaving between silent food trucks and closed vendor stalls. Every dark corner seemed like a potential hiding place for both the collar and whoever might have taken it.

A stack of empty crates created a narrow alley between two storage containers, and Pecan headed straight for it. The space smelled of damp cardboard and metal, with undertones of last night's rain still lingering in the shadows. Normally, he would have been sharing observations about who had passed through recently, picking up traces of thoughts and memories left behind. Now, all we had were his physical cues to follow.

"Start at the beginning," Jake said as we walked, his voice low and steady. "When did you last see him wearing it?"

I thought back to the previous evening, trying to piece together our last normal moments. "He had it when we closed up last night. We did our usual walk around the grounds before heading home." The memory of Pecan's last shared thoughts made my chest tight. He'd been commenting on how the carousel music always got stuck in his head, and how he was looking forward to our morning routine. "Everything was normal then."

A distant crash made us both jump. Just a vendor dropping supplies, but in our current state of heightened awareness, every unexpected sound felt threatening.

"He was wearing it when we passed Nina's cheese shop," I continued, trying to reconstruct our path. "He mentioned something about her thoughts being particularly worried about..." I stopped, realizing I was saying too much.

Jake didn't push, but his expression grew more thoughtful. "You know," he said carefully, examining a gap between containers, "I've noticed things. Little things that didn't quite add up. Like how you always seem to know when someone's about to cause trouble, or how Pecan reacts to conversations he shouldn't understand."

I froze, my hand hovering over a patch of trampled grass. "Jake..."

"I'm not pushing for answers," he said quickly, straightening up and holding his hands out in a peaceful gesture. "I just want you to know that whatever's going on, whatever that collar really means to you and Pecan, I'm here to help. No explanations needed." Before I could respond, Pecan barked again, this time with an urgency that drew both our attention. He was pawing at something partially hidden beneath one of the containers, his whole body tense with excitement.

Jake got down on his hands and knees, reaching into the narrow space. "There's definitely something here, but I can't quite... hang on." He stretched further, grunting with effort. "Got it!"

He pulled out a small cloth bag, the kind vendors used for merchandise. It was damp from the morning dew and slightly muddy, as if it had been hastily shoved under the container. Inside, we found a broken chain link, the kind used on Pecan's collar, and what looked like the remains of a torn festival security badge. The discovery sent a chill down my spine that had nothing to do with the morning air.

The security badge was torn diagonally, but I could make out part of a barcode and the edge of what might have been an official stamp. These badges were only issued to festival staff with after-hours access, people who could move around the grounds without drawing attention.

"Someone deliberately removed it," I said, my suspicion crystallizing into certainty. "They must have realized Pecan was helping with the investigation somehow. They knew exactly what they were looking for."

Jake examined the broken link, holding it up to catch the light. "This was cut, not broken. Look at the clean edge. Someone came prepared with tools. This wasn't a random act or an accident." He ran his thumb along the cut edge, his expression darkening. "These are professional cuts, Maple"

The implications sent another wave of cold fear through me. Without the collar, Pecan couldn't warn me about people's thoughts or intentions. We'd lost our advantage, and whoever took it knew exactly what they were doing.

The festival was fully awakening now.

His eyes scanned our surroundings with new wariness. "If someone's willing to go this far to interfere with your investigation..."

"They might not stop at stealing a dog collar," I finished. The syrup bottle in my pocket suddenly felt heavier.

Pecan pressed against my leg, offering comfort in the only way he could now.

"What do you want to do?" Jake asked, standing and brushing dirt from his knees.

I took a deep breath, trying to think clearly through my worry. "We need to find that collar. But we also need to figure out what Pecan was trying to tell us about this bottle. Someone at this festival is a murderer, and they're getting nervous enough to take action."

"Then we'll do both," Jake said firmly. "I'll help you search between customers today. And." He stopped.

"I know," I responded, heading back to the Waffle Wagon.

"If you want me to give it to Radcliffe, I will," he said.

I silently handed him the bottle, wondering if it was the death knell in my case.

Chapter 16

I stood in my Waffle Wagon, methodically arranging my supplies with the kind of focused attention usually reserved for defusing bombs.

Jake had done the right thing, turning that bottle over to Detective Radcliffe, but its absence left me feeling oddly untethered, like a balloon that had slipped its string. The physical proof of tampering, the one solid clue we'd managed to find, was now completely out of my control.

Pecan sat at attention near the prep counter, his eyes following my every movement with an intensity that made my heart ache. Without his collar, the usual stream of sarcastic commentary was absent, leaving a hollow space in my mind where his thoughts should have been. I missed his morning observations about the pigeons (*Honestly, they're just rats with better PR*) and his running commentary on early-morning vendors (*Oh look, Nina's wearing that awful sweater again, the one that makes her look like a deranged Christmas tree*).

"We're going to figure this out," I told him, more to fill the silence than anything else. He thumped his tail against the floor in response, and I could almost hear what he would have said: *Obviously. We're quite the team, even when one of us is temporarily muted.*

The familiar yellow paper of Grandpa Henry's recipe card sat propped against the mixer, though I hardly needed it anymore. Ancient batter stains marked the corners like sepia-toned memories, and his handwriting, precise yet somehow playful, brought a wave of comfort. What would he do in this situation? Probably something clever and slightly unorthodox, with a side of waffle-related wisdom.

I began mixing the day's first batch of batter, the wooden spoon creating hypnotic swirls in the bowl. Each step was muscle memory now, leaving my mind free to chase theories about who might have taken Pecan's collar and why.

The festival wouldn't open for another hour, giving me time for something I'd been avoiding: attempting to scry without Pecan's guidance. Setting aside the main batch of batter, I pulled out a clean bowl and poured a careful measure into it, watching as the surface settled into mirror-like stillness.

"Okay," I muttered, trying to center myself. "Focus, Maple."

Pecan padded over, resting his chin on my knee. I felt my breathing slow to match his. I focused on Felix, on his notebook full of secrets, on the mysterious "Sponsor" who seemed to lurk behind it all. The batter remained stubbornly still at first, showing nothing but my own uncertain reflection.

"Come on," I whispered, trying to channel whatever spark of magic had helped me before. "Show me something useful."

The surface rippled, ever so slightly, like a pond disturbed by a gentle breeze. Images flickered across it, faster than I could fully grasp, but each one leaving an impression.

Pecan's tail thumped against the floor, and he made a soft whining sound that seemed to say, *You're onto something here.* Even without his telepathic abilities, his encouragement was clear.

A sharp knock at the door made me jump, the bowl rattling against the counter. The images vanished like smoke, leaving only ordinary batter behind. My heart hammered against my ribs as if I'd been caught doing something illicit.

"Maple?" Jake's voice carried through the door. "You decent in there?"

I quickly set the scrying bowl aside, trying to calm my racing pulse. "Come on up!"

He climbed into the truck. His expression was carefully neutral, too neutral, which immediately set off warning bells in my head.

"What did Radcliffe say about the bottle?" I asked, trying to keep my voice casual as I returned to mixing the main batch of batter. The wooden spoon moved faster than necessary, betraying my anxiety.

Jake leaned against the counter, his fingers drumming an irregular pattern that spoke volumes about his discomfort. "Well..."

"That doesn't sound promising." I stopped stirring, watching his face for clues.

"He's... interested in it," Jake said slowly, choosing his words with obvious care. "But not necessarily in the way we hoped."

My stomach dropped like an elevator with cut cables. "What does that mean, exactly?"

"It means he's got questions about why you didn't turn it over immediately when you found it." Jake's expression softened, his eyes full of concern. "I tried to explain, but you know Radcliffe. He sees everything through cop-colored glasses."

I set down my mixing bowl with a force that sent a puff of flour into the air like a miniature explosion. "Of course he does. Because heaven forbid anything in this case be straightforward. Why would a potentially murderous food critic, mysterious blackmail schemes, and a stolen magical dog collar be simple?"

The words hung in the air between us, and I immediately regretted the outburst. Jake's eyebrows rose slightly at the mention of the magical collar, but true to his word, he didn't push for explanations.

Pecan pressed against my leg, offering silent support. Jake watched us both before breaking the tension with a gentle observation.

"You know," he said carefully, "I've been thinking about what you said earlier, about the collar being special." He paused, giving me space to elaborate if I wanted. When I remained silent, he continued, "Whatever it was, whatever it did, we'll find it. And in the meantime, you've got other skills. I saw you just now, with the bowl..."

I froze, my hand halfway to the flour container. "You did?"

He nodded, a slight smile playing at the corners of his mouth. "Through the window. I didn't want to interrupt right away. It look ed... important."

"I was just..." I gestured vaguely at the bowl of batter, searching for words that wouldn't make me sound completely unhinged. How do you explain to someone that you were trying to divine clues from eggs and flour?

"Hey," he held up his hands, "like I said before, no explanations needed. But did you... see anything useful?"

I considered the fragments I'd glimpsed, trying to piece them together like a jigsaw puzzle with most of the pieces missing. "Maybe.

But it was all so quick." I ran a hand through my hair, frustration building. "Without Pecan's help, it's like trying to tune a radio with mittens on."

"But you're still picking up signals," Jake pointed out. "That's something."

Outside, the festival grounds were stirring. Soon, the paths would be filled with people, all of them potential suspects or witnesses. The thought of facing them without Pecan's insights made my chest tight.

"I just feel like I'm losing my grip on everything," I admitted, measuring out flour. "The bottle's with Radcliffe, the collar's gone, and every time I think I'm getting closer to understanding what happened to Felix, something else slips away."

Jake was quiet for a moment, watching me work. Then he said, "You know what my dad always says about working on engines?"

"What's that?"

"Sometimes you have to stop looking at the whole machine and focus on one part at a time. Otherwise, you get overwhelmed by all the moving pieces."

I smiled despite myself, some of the tension easing from my shoulders. "Are you comparing murder investigation to auto repair?"

"If the wrench fits," he grinned, then grew serious again. "What's the one piece you can focus on right now?"

I thought about the images I'd seen in the batter, trying to isolate the clearest fragment. "The security uniform. Whoever took Pecan's collar had after-hours access to the festival grounds. But it was just a glimpse..."

"That's your starting point then," Jake said, straightening up with newfound purpose. "We can check the security schedule, see who was on duty last night."

"We?"

He pushed off from the counter. "I know most of the security team from doing maintenance on their golf carts. They talk while I work. You'd be amazed what people say when they think you're just focused on engines."

The festival's morning sounds were growing louder. Pecan's ears perked up at the increasing activity, his head turning to track each new sound. I remembered how he used to share snippets of vendors' thoughts as they set up: *Nina's worried about her cheese stock lasting the day. Mark's still angry about something – his thoughts are all red and spiky.*

"I should start getting ready to open," I said, reaching for my apron. "The morning rush will be here soon."

Jake nodded, heading for the door. "I'll ask around about the security schedules. And Maple?" He paused at the top step, his expression serious. "Whatever Radcliffe thinks about the bottle... Just... maybe don't go finding any more evidence without telling him first?"

"No promises," I said, smiling.

After Jake left, I threw myself into prep work, letting the familiar routine ground me.

The first customers began trickling in around eight, and I fell into the rhythm of pouring, cooking, and serving.

"You look tired, dear," Mrs. Henderson said, peering at me over her reading glasses. "Everything alright?"

"Just a busy festival," I replied, managing a smile as I poured batter onto the iron.

Between orders, I studied the festival security staff as they made their rounds. Their dark blue uniforms stood out against the cheerful festival decorations, and I tried to match each figure to the shadowy one I'd glimpsed in my scrying attempt. Nothing seemed obviously suspicious, but then again, whoever had taken Pecan's collar knew exactly what they were doing.

Around nine-thirty, Nina stopped by, her cheese shop apron already dusted with flour. "The usual, please," she said, then lowered her voice. "Any news about... you know?"

I shook my head slightly as I prepared her savory waffle. "Nothing concrete yet." I wanted to ask if she'd noticed anything unusual last night, but without Pecan's ability to read her thoughts, I couldn't be sure how much to trust her.

The morning crowd ebbed and flowed, faces blurring together in a parade of hungry festival-goers.

"I heard it was poison in the syrup," one woman whispered to her companion as they passed my window.

"No, no, it was in the waffle batter itself," her friend replied with authority. "That's why they're investigating the waffle vendor."

I gripped my spatula tighter, trying to ignore the gossip.

The morning crowd thinned around ten, giving me a brief respite. As I wiped down the counter, Pecan suddenly sat up straight, his attention fixed on something outside. Following his gaze, I spotted Detective Radcliffe making his way through the festival grounds, the evidence bottle carefully bagged and held in one hand.

My heart performed an uncomfortable gymnastics routine. This was it. Whatever he'd found, whatever conclusions he'd drawn, I was about to find out. Pecan's ears flattened slightly, and he moved closer to me. A silent guardian.

Radcliffe's expression was unreadable as he approached the Waffle Wagon, but there was something in his stride that made my stomach clench. The evidence bag caught the morning light, the glass bottle inside glinting like a warning signal.

I squared my shoulders and reached down to scratch Pecan's ears, drawing strength from his steady presence.

Radcliffe stopped at the bottom of my steps, his free hand resting on his belt near his badge. "Ms. Winslow," he said, his tone carefully neutral. "We need to talk about this bottle."

The festival continued around us, cheerful and oblivious, but in that moment, everything seemed to narrow down to just two things: the evidence bag in Radcliffe's hand and the growing certainty that whatever came next would change everything.

I took a deep breath. "Of course, Detective," I said, proud of how steady my voice sounded. "Would you like a waffle while we chat?"

His expression didn't change, but something flickered in his eyes. "This isn't a social call, Ms. Winslow."

"No," I agreed, meeting his gaze. "I suppose it isn't."

Chapter 17

The festival grounds around us buzzed with pre-judging activity, but all of that seemed muffled, distant, as Radcliffe fixed me with his stern gaze.

"Ms. Winslow," he began, his voice carrying the weight of official business, "after reviewing the evidence and conducting further interviews, I need you to come down to the station after the final judging."

The mixing bowl I'd been holding nearly slipped from my suddenly numb fingers. I set it down carefully, buying time to steady my voice. "Am I under arrest again?"

"Let's just say we have some serious questions that need answering in a more... formal setting." His eyes swept through my wagon, taking in the morning's prep work, the bowls of batter, the precisely measured ingredients, all the normal pieces of my life that now felt precarious. "The bottle you eventually turned in shows signs of tampering that match the toxicology report from Mr. Montclair's autopsy. The lab found traces of the same compound in both."

"I understand," I managed, proud that my voice remained steady despite the tremor in my hands. "What time should I expect to—"

"I'll come find you after the judging." Radcliffe's tone left no room for negotiation. He adjusted his stance, one hand resting near his badge. "Don't leave the festival grounds before then. And Ms. Winslow? I strongly suggest you don't try to investigate anything else on your own."

I turned back to my prep work, but my hands trembled as I measured ingredients. The festival handbook lay open on my counter, mocking me with its cheerful instructions about presentation and plating.

"Well, this is just perfect," I muttered to Pecan, who watched me with concerned eyes. "Grandpa Henry's legacy might end with me getting arrested for murder." I picked up a whisk, then set it down again, unable to focus. "What would he think of all this, huh? His granddaughter, suspected of poisoning a food critic at his beloved festival?"

The morning crowd ebbed and flowed around my wagon, their conversations drifting up to me in fragments:

"Did you hear about the critic?"

"Such a shame about Henry's granddaughter..."

Each whispered comment felt like a small cut.

The festival's head coordinator, Martha, bustled past with her ever-present clipboard, calling out reminders about the final judging. "Vendors, remember your presentation times! Three minutes each, no exceptions!"

I obsessed over every detail of my presentation waffle, as if perfect execution might somehow prove my innocence. My hands moved through the familiar motions while my mind raced with questions about what waited at the police station. Would there be formal charges? Would I need a lawyer? What would happen to the Waffle Wagon?

A gentle tap at my window startled me from my spiral of worry. Lucky stood there wearing what appeared to be at least three different floral patterns that somehow worked together.

"Maple, dear," she called softly, her eyes holding an urgency that seemed at odds with her whimsical appearance. "Might I have a word?"

I glanced at my half-finished prep work, then at the clock. The final judging loomed closer with each passing minute. "I've got about twenty minutes before—"

"This can't wait." Something in her tone made me pause. "Bring Pecan."

Curious despite my anxiety, I followed Lucky around the corner of my wagon, where a cluster of decorative shrubs provided a pocket of privacy. Lucky's bangles clinked softly as she reached into her voluminous bag, the kind that seemed to contain an entire universe of odds and ends, and pulled out something that made my heart stop.

Pecan's collar.

"How did you—" I began, but Lucky was already kneeling beside Pecan, her movements quick but gentle.

"The cards this morning showed me trouble," she explained, carefully fastening the collar around Pecan's neck. "Three of Swords reversed, followed by the Moon. Secrets and confusion. But then the Star appeared, and I knew I needed to follow my intuition." She patted Pecan's head, her voice dropping to a whisper. "Found this behind the maintenance shed, tucked under some tarps. Someone went to quite a bit of trouble to hide it. I had to fashion a makeshift clamp to fix it."

The moment the collar clicked into place, Pecan's thoughts exploded into my mind like fireworks at a Fourth of July celebration:

Oh, thank goodness I can finally tell you everything I've been trying to say for the past day and you wouldn't believe what I've heard and seen and smelled and there's something about the security guard that isn't right and did you know that Nina's cheese supplier is actually her ex-husband's cousin and Mark from the sauce stand has been sneaking extra samples when no one's looking and someone's been using the storage shed after hours and the pigeons have been acting weird and—

"Whoa, slow down!" I pressed my fingers to my temples, overwhelmed by the sudden rush of information. His thoughts came in a jumbled cascade.

Sorry, sorry, it's just been so frustrating not being able to tell you things and watching you worry and seeing Radcliffe act like you're some kind of criminal when really there's something much bigger going on here and I've been trying to bark hints but you humans are terrible at understanding bark-based communication and—

"Pecan, breathe," I instructed, then realized how ridiculous that sounded. "I mean, just... try to focus on one thing at a time."

Lucky watched our silent exchange with knowing eyes. "The connection might be a bit wobbly at first," she said, her voice carrying the weight of experience. "Like any channel of communication, it needs time to settle after being disrupted. Think of it like tuning an old radio. Sometimes you have to wait for the static to clear."

She's right. Everything feels sort of fizzy, like seltzer water in my brain, Pecan admitted. *But Maple, there's something important about last night. I saw—*

His thoughts suddenly scattered like startled birds, fragments of images and impressions flashing through our connection too quickly to grasp.

"It's okay," I soothed, though worry gnawed at my stomach.

Lucky touched my arm gently, her rings cool against my skin. "Don't force it, dear. The universe has its own timing." She glanced toward the festival's main area, where vendors were gathering for the final judging. "Speaking of timing, you should probably get back to your preparations. But remember. Sometimes what seems like an ending is really just a different kind of beginning."

The festival's morning bustle had grown louder, more urgent. Martha's voice carried across the grounds again, calling out the final warning for final presentations.

I wanted to ask Lucky more about finding the collar, about what else her cards might have shown, but she was right. The final judging wouldn't wait, and I still had work to do. Besides, Detective Radcliffe's warning loomed over everything like a storm cloud. Whatever happened at the judging, I'd be heading to the police station afterward.

Back in my wagon, I tried to focus on perfecting my presentation while simultaneously sorting through Pecan's scattered thoughts. If it was the last thing I did with my freedom, I would make Grandpa Henry proud.

The security guard was wearing different shoes, Pecan suddenly announced, the thought cutting through the chaos like a spotlight through fog. *The boots were wrong.*

"Wrong how?" I asked, carefully drizzling honey over my waffle creation in a pattern Grandpa Henry had taught me years ago.

I don't know exactly. It's all blurry, like trying to remember a dream about bacon. His frustration colored the thought, making it wobble. *But it's important somehow. And there was something about the maintenance shed... something that didn't belong...*

I added a final garnish to my plate, trying to keep my hands steady as I processed this information. The festival grounds had gotten quieter, that peculiar hush that falls before something important. "Keep working on it. Maybe if we—"

"Let the judging begin!" Martha's voice rang out, making me jump and nearly sending my carefully arranged plate flying.

We'll figure this out, Pecan's thought came through clearer now, tinged with determination. *I may be a bit scrambled right now, but I'm still your partner in crime-solving. Also, the judge on the left had sardines for breakfast, which seems highly suspicious.*

"Crime-solving, not crime-committing," I reminded him, gathering my presentation plate and checking my apron for stains. "Though I'm not sure Detective Radcliffe sees the difference."

Radcliffe needs to get his head out of his case files and look at what's really happening, Pecan grumbled. *Also, his socks don't match today, which really undermines his authority. And he's thinking about his grocery list, which includes cat food, so at least we know he has a heart.*

Despite everything, I felt a smile tugging at my lips. Having Pecan's running commentary back in my head was like finding my balance again, even if our connection wasn't quite at full strength.

Chapter 18

I watched through the Waffle Wagon's serving window as Avery Mullen approached. The morning sun caught his perfectly coiffed silver hair, and his forest green bow tie sat at a precise angle that spoke of countless minutes spent before a mirror.

Here comes Mr. Fancy Pants himself, Pecan's thoughts drifted up to me. *And his mind is all jumbled up like a basket of tangled leashes.*

My hands trembled slightly as I put the finishing touches on my competition waffle, a savory three-cheese blend with herbs de Provence and a honey-lavender drizzle. Detective Radcliffe's warning from earlier still echoed in my mind: after the judging, I'd be heading to the police station for formal questioning. Everything hinged on these next few moments.

Avery stopped at my window, his expression a carefully constructed mask of polite interest. Behind him, a small crowd had gathered, eager to watch one of the festival's most influential judges sample my creation.

"Ah, Ms. Winslow," he said, making my name sound simultaneously like a compliment and an accusation. "I trust you're prepared for the final judging?"

"Of course," I replied, sliding my carefully plated waffle onto the serving ledge. "A savory three-cheese waffle with herbs de Provence and a honey-lavender drizzle, inspired by my grandfather's original recipe."

Avery nodded, producing a small glass bottle from his jacket pocket with the flourish of a magician revealing his favorite trick. "You'll forgive me, but I always prefer to use my own syrup. A particular... preference of mine."

The moment the bottle appeared, Pecan's thoughts exploded in my head. *That bottle! Maple, that bottle! The smell. It's exactly like the one I found behind the maintenance shed! The same bitter undertone, the same fancy label, even the same scratch on the cap where someone. Wait, everything's connecting now!*

My heart raced as I watched Avery uncap the syrup.

His thoughts just went dark, Pecan reported urgently. *Like storm clouds rolling in. He's remembering something about Felix and the maintenance shed, but he's trying to block it out.*

"Your own bottle," I said carefully, watching Avery's manicured hands as he prepared to pour. "Custom blend?"

"Family recipe," he replied smoothly, though I noticed a slight tremor in his grip. "Been using it for years. One must maintain certain standards in this industry."

The syrup drizzled onto my waffle, and I caught another whiff of that telltale bitterness. My mind raced, connecting dots like a detective's string board.

"Funny," I continued, keeping my voice low but firm. "I recently came across a very similar bottle. Had an unusual bitter note to it. Almost like... almonds?"

Avery's hand jerked slightly, sending a splash of syrup onto the plate's rim. "I'm not sure what you're implying, Ms. Winslow, but I suggest you focus on your presentation rather than making wild accusations."

His heart rate just spiked like a squirrel spotting a hawk, Pecan reported. *And he's thinking about his passport. Who thinks about their passport during a waffle judging?*

The morning crowd had grown quieter, sensing the tension building between us. Even Martha had paused her clipboard activities to watch.

"Felix Montclair was known for his particular tastes too, wasn't he?" I pressed, watching Avery's composed facade crack ever so slightly. "And his tendency to use that knowledge to his advantage? The festival circuit can be quite competitive, after all. So many reputations at stake, so many secrets to keep."

"This is hardly the time or place—" Avery began, his knuckles white around the syrup bottle.

"He was blackmailing you, wasn't he?" I kept my voice steady despite my racing heart. "Threatening to expose your little bribery scheme? I imagine a judge's reputation is worth quite a lot in the culinary world. Worth killing for, maybe?"

Oh, that hit a nerve, Pecan's thoughts crackled with tension. *His mind just exploded with guilt and panic. He's remembering watching Felix take that first bite, waiting for the poison to work.*

"You're just a food truck vendor," Avery hissed, leaning closer to my window. "You have no idea what it takes to survive in this industry. The politics, the favors, the constant pressure to—" He caught himself, but his eyes darted to the syrup bottle and back.

"How many positive reviews did you sell over the years, Mr. Mullen?" I continued, my voice barely above a whisper. "How many careers did you make or break based on who could pay the most? Felix must have had quite a file on you."

Avery's face flushed red, spreading from his neck to his hairline. "You don't understand," he spat. "Felix pushed too far, demanded too much. He was going to ruin everything I'd built. Twenty years of reputation, of influence, all because he thought he could—" He stopped abruptly, realizing what he'd revealed.

Got him! Pecan's mental voice was triumphant. *His thoughts are screaming 'guilty' now. Also, he's calculating the distance to the north parking lot. And something about papers he needs to destroy.*

The crowd had grown larger, drawn by the mounting tension. Martha stepped forward, her clipboard clutched to her chest. "Is everything alright here? Perhaps we should take a brief—"

"Just fine," Avery cut her off, standing straighter and adjusting his bow tie with trembling fingers. "I simply need some air. This... atmosphere is rather stifling."

"Mr. Mullen," I said, my voice carrying clearly despite the crowd's murmur. "The police will be very interested in that syrup bottle. And I'm sure they'll find it matches the traces they found in Felix's system. Just like the bottle that was hidden behind the maintenance shed."

He's going to run, Pecan warned. *His fight-or-flight response is definitely leaning toward flight. And he's thinking about back roads to avoid the highway.*

For a moment, Avery stood frozen, his carefully maintained dignity warring with panic. Then, like a cornered animal, he made his choice. He shoved past my serving window with surprising strength, knocking over a display of local honey jars in his wake.

"Stop him!" Martha's voice rang out, but Avery was already pushing through the crowd, his silver hair bobbing through the sea of people like a beacon.

He's heading for the north lot! Pecan's thoughts spurred me into action. *And he's thinking about the papers in his glove compartment, evidence of all his bribes and blackmail payments!*

I vaulted over my serving counter, ignoring the gasps from the crowd. My heart pounded as I realized this was it. The moment to prove my innocence and bring Felix's killer to justice.

"Come on, Pecan," I called, already moving. "We've got a judge to catch."

Finally, some action! Pecan bounded ahead of me, his tail wagging with excitement. *Though I should point out that chasing suspicious humans is significantly less satisfying than chasing squirrels. They rarely climb trees, and they tend to use cars, which is just cheating.*

We burst into the morning sunshine, the festival grounds a maze of vendors and visitors. Ahead, I could see Avery pushing his way through the crowd, his bow tie now askew and his perfect hair beginning to wilt in the humidity.

He's thinking about his car keys, Pecan reported as we ran. *Left pocket. And he's regretting wearing those expensive leather shoes today. Finally, someone else's footwear choices are causing them problems!*

The sound of running feet and shouting voices filled the air as we raced through the festival grounds. The peaceful morning transformed into chaos by one man's desperate bid for freedom. But this time, the truth wouldn't stay buried under layers of secrets and lies. This time, justice would be served. With or without syrup.

Avery darted between two food trucks, knocking over a stack of empty boxes in his wake. The crash sent several festival-goers jumping backward, creating a temporary barrier between us. I swerved around the obstacle course of scattered cardboard and startled onlookers, keeping his silver hair in sight.

He's thinking about a backup plan, Pecan reported, easily keeping pace beside me. *Something about a storage locker in Portland. And he's got cash stashed in his spare tire. Who keeps money in their tire? That's just asking for mold issues.*

The festival grounds had transformed into a chaotic maze of vendors and visitors, most of whom seemed torn between getting out of our way and trying to capture the scene on their phones.

"Excuse me! Sorry! Coming through!" I called out, dodging around a family with matching waffle t-shirts. The father still held his half-eaten breakfast, fork frozen halfway to his mouth as he watched the chase unfold.

Ahead, Avery knocked over a display of artisanal maple products, sending bottles rolling across the ground like wooden bowling pins. The vendor's cry of dismay mixed with the general chaos, adding another layer to the morning's unexpected symphony.

Watch out for that puddle of syrup! Pecan warned. *Though I must say, there's a certain poetic justice in him being brought down by his own preferred condiment.*

Chapter 19

"Security to the main thoroughfare!" Martha's voice carried across the grounds, her usual clipboard-wielding authority now tinged with genuine alarm.

Avery's perfectly pressed slacks were now stained with mud at the cuffs, his designer shoes leaving distinctive prints in the soft ground. He knocked over a display of artisanal jams, sending glass jars rolling across our path like crystalline bowling balls.

Duck right! Pecan warned. *And mind that raspberry preserve. Though I must say, it smells delicious. Is this really the time to be thinking about breakfast? Yes, yes it is.*

I swerved around the spreading pool of jam, my heart pounding with each step.

"Mr. Mullen!" I called out, trying to keep my voice steady despite my labored breathing. "You're only making things worse!"

The crowd of festival-goers called out encouragement. "Get him, Maple!" "Don't let him get away!"

He's getting tired, Pecan observed. *His thoughts are getting sluggish, like a squirrel after finding an entire pizza crust. Speaking of which, remember when I found that pizza last week? Good times.*

"Focus, Pecan!" I gasped, dodging around a pottery display. "Where's he heading?"

Right now? He's thinking about the service entrance behind the main pavilion. There's a delivery van he's hoping to hide behind. Also, he's really regretting that extra helping of eggs Benedict this morning. Breakfast revenge is real.

I could hear snippets of conversation as we passed: "Isn't that the fancy judge?" "What's going on?" "Did you see his bow tie? It's completely crooked!"

"Stop him!" A voice called out from the crowd. "He's been taking bribes for years!"

The accusation seemed to hit Avery like a physical blow. He stumbled slightly, his rhythm breaking just enough for me to gain a few feet on him.

As we rounded the corner of the pavilion, I caught sight of the service entrance Pecan had mentioned. Avery was making a desperate sprint for it, his bow tie now completely undone and fluttering behind him like a surrender flag that refused to wave.

"Mr. Mullen!" I called out, my voice carrying across the distance between us. "The evidence is already there. You can't run from this!"

He's thinking about burning something, Pecan reported urgently. *Files in his car, records of payments, a whole network of—wait, someone's coming. Someone angry. Really angry.*

Just then, a familiar figure stepped out from behind a food truck, directly in Avery's path. Sassy Bright stood with her arms crossed, her usual perfectly styled hair slightly windswept but her expression fierce and determined. Her crepe truck's logo glinted on her apron, a queen's crown now looking more like a battle helmet.

"Going somewhere, Avery?" she asked, her voice carrying years of accumulated rage. "Or are you finally running out of vendors to terrorize?"

Avery skidded to a halt, his designer shoes sliding on the dewy grass. His head whipped from side to side, looking for an escape route, but the gathering crowd had formed a loose circle around us. Vendors who had been setting up their morning displays now abandoned their tasks to join the growing audience.

His thoughts just went into complete meltdown, Pecan commented. *Like a squirrel discovering all the bird feeders have suddenly become squirrel-proof. Though I still think those feeders are just a challenge, not a prevention.*

"This is ridiculous," Avery said, attempting to straighten his disheveled appearance. "You're all overreacting to a simple misunderstanding. Felix was the one behind everything. I was merely trying to maintain order in the festival circuit."

"Order?" Sassy took a step forward, her voice trembling with emotion. "Is that what you call it? Because I remember you and Felix cornering me at the Portland Food Festival last year, threatening to write about 'questionable hygiene practices' unless I paid up."

The crowd's murmuring grew louder, and I could see several vendors nodding in recognition. Nina pushed her way forward, her usually cheerful face set in hard lines.

"You threatened my entire business," she called out, her voice clear and strong. "Said you'd write about health code violations that didn't exist unless I paid your 'consulting fee.' Three thousand dollars a month! Do you know how many wheels of artisanal cheese I had to sell to cover that?"

"And my crepe stand," another vendor shouted, stepping forward. His white chef's coat was spotted with batter, but his eyes blazed with righteous anger. "You said my technique was 'tragically amateur' until I slipped you that envelope full of cash. Then suddenly I was 'showing promise.'"

The guilt in his head is getting louder, Pecan observed. *Like a whole pack of dogs barking at once. Also, he's calculating distances to every possible exit. Not that I'm letting him get past me. I've chased too many squirrels to let a human outrun me.*

Avery's composed facade crumbled completely as the accusations flew. His eyes darted around like a trapped animal's, and I could see the moment he made one final, desperate attempt at escape. His hand moved toward his pocket, where I caught a glimpse of something metallic.

"Don't even think about it," I warned, stepping closer. "Whatever you're reaching for, it's not worth adding another charge to your list."

It's just his phone, Pecan assured me. *Though he was briefly considering throwing it as a distraction. His strategic thinking isn't great under pressure. Unlike me. I once faked left AND right to catch a particularly clever chipmunk.*

"You don't understand," Avery's voice cracked, his carefully cultivated accent slipping. "The pressure in this industry, the constant competition. Felix knew how to play the game. He understood that success required... management."

"You mean extortion," I corrected, keeping my voice steady. "How long were you two working together? How many careers did you destroy because someone couldn't afford your protection racket?"

"Remember the Summer Feast last year?" A woman in a baker's apron called out. "My sourdough booth? You said my bread was 'distressingly dense' until I agreed to your 'mentorship program.'"

"The Holiday Market!" Another voice joined in. "You threatened to expose my family recipe unless I paid for your silence!"

Each accusation seemed to hit Avery like a physical blow, causing him to shrink further into himself.

He's about to break, Pecan reported. *His thoughts are all jumbled now, like a dropped box of puzzle pieces.*

"It wasn't supposed to end like this," Avery said, his voice suddenly small and tired. "Felix was pushing too hard, demanding more than his share. Twenty years of building my reputation, all the connections I'd made, the influence I'd gained. He was going to destroy it all."

"So you decided to destroy him first," I finished, taking another careful step forward. "Used your position as a judge to get close, knowing he'd never suspect the syrup bottle. You probably thought it was the perfect crime. Blame it on the new vendor, the outsider trying to make a name for herself."

The crowd had grown silent now, hanging on every word. Phones were still recording, capturing every moment of Avery's breakdown. In the distance, I could hear sirens approaching, growing louder with each passing second.

Detective Radcliffe is coming, Pecan confirmed. *His thoughts are very... determined. And slightly smug.*

"I had no choice!" Avery's voice rose to a shout, echoing across the suddenly silent festival grounds. "He was going to ruin everything! All my hard work, my reputation, my influence. Gone because of his greed!"

"You had a choice," Sassy said quietly, her words carrying across the hushed crowd. "We all did. Some of us chose to stand up to the bullying, even if it meant taking a hit to our businesses. Others chose to pay up and stay quiet. But you? You chose murder."

The sound of footsteps drew everyone's attention as Detective Radcliffe finally pushed through the last row of onlookers, his badge catching the morning light. Two uniformed officers flanked him, their expressions grim but professional.

"That's quite a confession, Mr. Mullen," Radcliffe said, producing a pair of handcuffs. "Would you like to continue this discussion down at the station?"

Finally! Pecan's thought was triumphant. *Though I have to say, human justice involves an awful lot of paperwork. In the dog world, we just chase the troublemakers until they learn their lesson. Much more efficient.*

"You don't understand," Avery tried one last time, his voice breaking. "The festival circuit... it's a different world. We had a system. Everything was under control until Felix got greedy."

"Under control?" I stepped forward, my voice clear and steady. "You mean you had everyone under your thumb. But you forgot something important about food, Mr. Mullen. Something my grandfather taught me."

Avery's eyes met mine, and for a moment, I saw a flicker of genuine curiosity beneath his desperation.

"Real food, good food, brings people together," I continued, gesturing to the crowd around us. "It creates communities, builds trust, shares joy. What you and Felix did? That destroyed everything food is supposed to represent."

Oh, that was good, Pecan approved. *Though you forgot to mention treats. Treats are very important to community building. Just saying.*

Detective Radcliffe stepped forward, the handcuffs ready. "Avery Mullen, you're under arrest for the murder of Felix Montclair and multiple counts of extortion." He began.

The click of the handcuffs seemed to break some invisible tension in the air. The crowd burst into spontaneous applause.

"Way to go, Maple!" someone shouted from the crowd.

"Justice for the vendors!" another voice called out.

You did it, Pecan thought proudly. *Though I helped. A lot. I deserve at least three treats for this. Maybe four, considering all the running. Actually, let's make it five. I did some excellent mind-reading under pressure.*

Sassy approached me, her hand extended and a genuine smile replacing her usual competitive smirk. "Thank you," she said warmly. "For bringing all of this into the light. It's been going on for too long."

I took her hand, feeling years of rivalry dissolve into something that felt surprisingly like friendship. "Thank you for stepping in when you did. I couldn't have cornered him without your help."

Next time, Pecan thought contentedly, *maybe we could solve a mystery that doesn't involve so much running? I mean, I'm excellent at it, obviously, but I prefer my adventures to be more food-focused.*

Chapter 20

Detective Radcliffe cleared his throat, commanding attention from the gathered crowd. The handcuffed Avery Mullen had already been escorted to a waiting patrol car, leaving behind a wake of whispers and relieved sighs.

Pecan mused, sitting regally beside me. *His running form was an insult to four-legged creatures everywhere. And did you see how he knocked over those jam jars? Complete amateur. I would have at least sampled them first.*

I stifled a laugh, grateful for my furry friend's ability to lighten even the tensest moments. Detective Radcliffe's usual stern expression had softened somewhat as he addressed the crowd. "Based on recent evidence and Mullen's confession, Maple Winslow is no longer a suspect in this investigation." He gave me a curt nod, as if the gesture physically pained him. "Her... assistance helped resolve this case."

The crowd erupted in cheers, and I felt my cheeks flush with warmth. Nina wrapped me in a tight hug, while Sassy gave me a thumbs up from her crepe truck.

You're turning the color of a perfectly toasted waffle, Pecan observed, tail wagging. *Though personally, I think you deserve all the attention. We make quite the detective duo. Speaking of which, I believe this calls for celebratory treats. At least seven. No, eight. I did extra running today.*

Martha pushed through the crowd, her clipboard now wielded more like a conductor's baton than a weapon of organizational warfare.

"The Waffle Festival will continue as planned," she announced. "And I believe we have some special recognition in order. Maple Winslow, would you please step forward?"

"Oh, that's really not necessary," I protested. Jake appeared at the edge of my vision, giving me an encouraging nod that somehow made my heart flutter despite the morning's chaos.

Martha said, "A certificate will follow later. But in the meantime, we have a new award. The Most Innovative Festival Creation." Martha pulled something from her pocket. A small golden waffle-shaped pin that caught the morning light. I knew Grandpa Henry would be proud.

He'd be prouder if you added bacon, Pecan suggested helpfully. *Everything's better with bacon. That should be your next innovation. Though maybe we should wait until after all the murder accusations are fully cleared up. Just saying.*

The applause that followed felt genuine. As the crowd dispersed, returning to their booths and breakfast plans, I noticed Ellie Thistlewood hovering at the edge of the gathering. Her usually cheerful face carried a weight I hadn't noticed before.

"Maple, dear," she said softly as I approached. "Would you mind if we had a word? Somewhere quiet?" Her voice trembled slightly.

Pecan shared gently. *Her thoughts are all mixed up and sad. Also, she has cookies in her pocket, but I don't think now's the time to mention that.*

We found a bench beneath an old oak tree, its leaves creating dappled shadows that danced across Ellie's face. Pecan settled at my feet, unusually subdued.

Pecan shared gently. *Her thoughts are full of memories. The kind that make humans want to look at old photographs and cry into tea cups.*

"I need to tell you something," Ellie began, her voice barely above a whisper. Her hands trembled as she reached into her apron pocket.

"About Felix." She pulled out a worn photograph, its edges soft from years of handling. "He was my son."

The revelation hit me like a sudden gust of wind, stealing my breath for a moment. I studied the photograph – a younger Ellie stood beside a teenage boy with familiar features. They were standing in front of what looked like a small bakery, a "Grand Opening" banner partially visible in the background.

"That was his first job," Ellie explained, noticing where my gaze had landed. "He was sixteen, so excited about learning the business. He had such dreams then, such passion for food and writing." Her finger traced the outline of young Felix's face. "I watched him change over the years, from that bright, passionate boy to someone I barely recognized."

"But why didn't you ever tell him?" I asked softly, trying to reconcile this new information with everything I knew about Felix Montclair, the feared food critic who had terrorized so many vendors.

Ellie's laugh was hollow, like wind through an empty house. "I kept hoping if I stayed close enough, volunteered at enough festivals, maybe I could reach him somehow." Her voice cracked. "But I was too much of a coward to even tell him who I was. How do you tell someone you're the mother who gave them up? That you've been watching from the shadows of their life, seeing every mistake, every wrong turn, and doing nothing?"

There's so much regret in her thoughts, Pecan observed.

"I was young," Ellie continued, her words coming faster now, like a dam breaking. "Barely eighteen when I had him. No money, no support system, nothing to offer a child. The adoption agency promised he'd go to a good home, with opportunities I couldn't give him." She dabbed at her eyes with the corner of her apron. "And he did, at first. The Montclairs were wealthy, respected. I thought I'd made the right choice."

"What changed?" I asked, though part of me already suspected the answer.

"Money," Ellie said simply. "The Montclairs lost everything in a bad investment when Felix was in college. He had to drop out, take whatever work he could find. That's when he started writing reviews. Small pieces at first, then bigger ones as he realized he could profit from people's fear of bad publicity."

"I'm not sorry he was caught," Ellie said firmly, surprising me with the sudden steel in her voice. "What he did, what he became, was wrong. But I am sorry I never found the courage to try and help him change course." She squeezed my hand, her baker's calluses rough against my skin. "Thank you for seeking the truth, Maple. Even if it wasn't the ending I hoped for."

She means it, Pecan confirmed.

"What will you do now?" I asked gently.

Ellie tucked the photograph away, smoothing her apron with practiced hands. "Keep baking. Keep volunteering. The festival needs its cookie lady." She managed a small smile. "And maybe start a scholarship fund in Felix's name, for young food writers who need a little help staying on the right path."

As Ellie walked away, her shoulders straighter than before, I felt a new appreciation for how complicated justice could be. Maybe I should tell her that Felix was taking money to pay someone's medical bills. I wonder if that might give her some peace?

I finally returned to the Waffle Wagon. The day's events had left me exhausted but oddly peaceful.

Jake approached with two steaming cups of coffee and that crooked smile that always made my heart skip. He'd changed from his morning clothes into fresh jeans and a soft flannel shirt.

"Thought you might need this," he said, holding out a cup. "It's been quite a day."

Oh good, Jake's here, Pecan's tail wagged enthusiastically. *Maybe he brought treats. He seems like someone who would understand the importance of treats after solving a murder.*

We settled on the small steps of the Waffle Wagon, our shoulders touching comfortably as the festival wound down around us. The coffee was perfect, strong and sweet, just like I needed.

"Did you catch up to Detective Radcliffe?" I asked. With Avery's arrest, I hoped that put any guilt towards me to bed.

"Yeah, he wouldn't say much. But he did share that Avery poisoned Felix's syrup bottle with some type of special spice that he used in his own. That's what was making the bitter odor."

"Wow. To take someone's personal information and use it against them," I said.

Diabolical, Pecan's thoughts chimed in, *and Avery stole that security guard's badge to make all of that happen at night.I*

"So," Jake began carefully, turning his coffee cup in his hands. "About earlier, during the chase. I could have sworn I heard you talking to Pecan like he was answering you. And not just the usual dog-owner chat. It was like... like you were having an actual conversation."

I froze mid-sip, feeling my pulse quicken. The moment I'd been both anticipating and dreading had arrived. The festival lights were twinkling on around us, creating a strangely intimate atmosphere for such a potentially awkward conversation.

Just tell him the truth, Pecan suggested, settling himself between us. *He already likes you. I can tell by the way his thoughts get all fuzzy when he looks at you. Plus, if he doesn't believe you, I can always think really loud about that secret Justin Bieber song he likes to sing in his truck when he thinks no one's listening.*

"Jake," I started, then paused, trying to find the right words. How exactly does one explain supernatural pet communication to a practical-minded mechanic? "What would you say if I told you that som etimes... magical things happen in Starfall Glen?"

He raised an eyebrow but didn't pull away. "Magical things?"

"Like, for instance," I continued, focusing on my coffee cup, "a very special antique dog collar that might enable certain telepathic conversations with a particularly opinionated Tibetan Terrier?"

The festival sounds faded into background noise as I waited for his response.

His thoughts are actually pretty calm, Pecan reported. *Though he's wondering if this explains why I always seem to know when he's got beef jerky in his pocket. Which, by the way, he does right now.*

Jake was quiet for a moment, studying Pecan who gave his most innocent tail wag in return. Then he smiled.

"You know what?" he said finally. "That actually explains a lot. Like how you always seem to know things you couldn't possibly know during your investigations. Or why Pecan gives me that knowing look whenever I'm thinking about asking you out."

Ha! I knew he noticed those looks. I practiced them in the mirror and everything.

Relief flooded through me, and I leaned slightly closer to Jake. "You're taking this surprisingly well."

"Maple," he chuckled, "I've lived in Starfall Glen my whole life. I've seen the way your grandfather's old recipes seem to make people fall in love, how Martha's festival clipboard appears to defy the laws of physics, and how Lucky's antique shop items always seem to find exactly the right owner at exactly the right time." He shrugged. "A telepathic dog? That's actually one of the more reasonable explanations I've heard." He chuckled.

I like him even more now, Pecan declared. *He's smart. Plus, he still has that beef jerky in his pocket.*

"There's something else you should know," I said, sobering slightly. "Felix wasn't working alone. That reference we saw in Felix's notebook of someone called 'The Sponsor' pulling strings from the shadows."

Jake's expression grew serious as he shifted to face me more directly. “Do you know who it is?”

There had only been rumors swirling. “Some of the older vendors mentioned a pattern going back years before Felix even started his reviewing career. Someone on the town council, using the festival circuit to manipulate outcomes for their own benefit."

"With Avery's confession, they'll probably go to ground," Jake continued. "But something tells me this isn't over."

Definitely not, Pecan agreed, his ears perking up. *Though maybe our next mystery could involve fewer food critics and more pet-friendly establishments.*

"So, I have a question. Can Pecan hear my thoughts, too?" Jake asked.

Pecan grinned from ear to ear.

"Well, then, can he tell us who took his collar?" Jake asked.

Pecan tucked his head. I laughed. "It actually turns out that he got it caught on something and ended up slipping out of it."

Hey, I thought that was pretty clever.

Jake's voice softened as he set his empty cup aside. "Maybe we could focus on something a little less mysterious?" He turned to face me fully, and I could see a hint of nervousness. "Would you maybe like to have dinner with me tomorrow? And maybe take in that production at the local theater?"

"I'd love that," I replied.

Finally! Pecan flopped dramatically onto his side. *I thought he'd never ask. Though I hope you realize this means I'll need to approve the restaurant. And the menu. And possibly his entire wardrobe.*

As Jake left for the evening, Pecan suddenly bolted upright, nose twitching with purpose. Before I could stop him, he darted into the Waffle Wagon, the sound of his nails clicking against the floor accompanied by what seemed like determined rummaging.

Found it! he declared triumphantly, emerging with something clutched gently in his mouth. *It was behind that box of waffle mix you never use because it's not as good as Grandpa Henry's recipe.*

He dropped an old photograph at my feet, and I picked it up carefully, brushing away a light coating of flour. The image showed my grandfather Henry standing beside a striking woman I didn't recognize. They both held what looked like matching antique pendants.

Something about the woman's face tugged at my memory. The way she held herself, the knowing look in her eyes. It reminded me of someone, but I couldn't quite place who.

There's writing on the back, Pecan noted, nosing the photograph. *And before you ask, no, I can't read it. Being telepathic doesn't mean I suddenly understand human squiggles.*

I turned it over, finding faded handwriting that read: "Henry and V. - Guardians of the Glen, 1962." Below that, in even fainter script: "The key lies in the heart of what was lost."

"Guardians of the Glen?" I murmured, feeling a familiar tingle of mystery stirring in my chest. "What do you think that means?"

Well, Pecan settled beside me, resting his head on my knee, *I think it means we've found our next adventure. But first, can we please have dinner? Solving murders really works up an appetite. And Jake still has that beef jerky in his pocket that he completely forgot to share.*

I tucked the photograph safely into my apron pocket, knowing it would wait for another day. For now, I was content to sit with my loyal companion.

About the Author

Hello from the cozy corners of my imagination! I'm Sue Hollowell. If we were meeting in person, you'd probably find me offering you a slice of cake (extra frosting, because life's too short!) and reminiscing about the playful antics of my beloved spaniels.

Having an empty nest filled me with an abundance of memories and affection, looking for an outlet. With time on my hands and a head full of stories, I ventured into the enchanting realm of writing.

I write cozy mysteries featuring charming small-town settings, delightful characters, and a mix of mystery and whimsy. My stories often involve courageous amateur sleuths, beloved pets, and a sense of community, making them perfect for readers who enjoy lighthearted and engaging mysteries.

Stay tuned, and get ready to dive into worlds filled with mystery, charm, and more than a few surprises.

Milton Keynes UK
Ingram Content Group UK Ltd.
UKHW030805071224
452128UK00003B/161

9 798230 447429